LOVEHANDLES

Other books by Holly Jacobs:

Pickup Lines

LOVEHANDLES

•

Holly Jacobs

AVALON BOOKS
NEW YORK

PRINTED IN THE UNITED STATES OF AMERICA
ON ACID-FREE PAPER
BY HADDON CRAFTSMEN, BLOOMSBURG, PENNSYLVANIA

For Michelle Grajkowski . . . Thanks for the support.

And for Classy 100's Breakfast Club,
thanks for everything.

Chapter One

"This is WLVH Lovehandles, where love is more than just a song," a deep baritone announced. "It's two o'clock on the nose, and speaking about noses, we're here to watch a man be led around by one—"

"Punch," came an amused female voice with a tsk for punctuation. "Stop the commentating."

"Fine, I'll stop. This is the non-commentating Punch O'Brien—"

"—and Judy Bently. Saturdays aren't our normal spot, but today is special. We're here with our first live wedding broadcast."

"Weddings." His less than enthusiastic opinion of weddings was evident in that one word. No one in the radio audience could miss it. Judy was the only one, however, treated to the expression that accompanied that one-worded opinion; it added a definite exclamation point of disgust.

Peter "Punch" O'Brien had a face that made the female population drool, and even his current expression of distaste—bordering on a scowl—couldn't mar his chiseled features. If anything, it gave him a dark, dangerous air that made him even more attractive . . . if a woman liked that kind of thing.

Fortunately, Judy didn't.

She might be the only female over the age of ten and under the age of ninety in Erie, Pennsylvania whose head didn't turn when Peter walked into a room. After a year of working with him, she was immune to his looks.

As Peter shook his head, a single piece of charcoal hair shifted. Judy didn't feel the slightest urge to push it back into place . . . well, hardly the slightest urge.

He chose that moment to push the unruly strand back into place himself, saving Judy the trouble.

"Weddings," he scoffed again, "They're only for fools and dreamers."

"Not today, Punch," Judy scolded on air. Her role in their on-air partnership was that of *mom*. She scolded, nagged, and in general acted shocked when Peter acted up and played his "Punch" role to the hilt.

Today it wasn't much of an act. She was getting

tired of his anti-marriage prattle—almost as tired as she was with her role as mother.

She didn't want to play a role at the wedding other than that of guest. She just wanted to enjoy the day. It was a day that had started out full of promise.

A day Peter seemed bound and determined to ruin with his anti-marriage discourse.

This morning, Judy's normally unruly chestnut curls had decided to behave and remain in at least some semblance of a style, as if they sensed that the day was important. She tugged at her five-year-old beige sheath. She hated wearing dresses. She never felt she quite pulled them off, but today she felt she looked good.

Yes, the day had started off full of promise. Well-behaved hair, half-way decent dress and a wedding. Judy was a sucker for a wedding. All in all, she had looked forward to a perfect day. She'd simply forgotten to take her partner into consideration.

Peter snorted his disgust. "For those of you who weren't around this summer, you missed a real scorcher. Ethan and Mary spent two weeks living in a brand new Chevy truck, part of a contest sponsored by Lovehandles and Big Al's Autos."

He waved his hand and Judy took over the on-air dialogue. "Ethan won the truck. But later we found out he won more than just that—he won the heart of our Mary as well."

The back of the church stirred and Judy's voice

dropped to a whisper. "And the organ is starting to play the processional. Here comes Mary. She's wearing a traditional white dress, looking like Cinderella come to life. It's simple silk covered with miles of lace."

She sighed. Mary looked like every little girl's fantasy.

"Seems our Judy has a romantic streak." Peter's tone suggested that having a romantic streak was a terrible curse, and one by which he'd never be afflicted. "All I see when I look at Mary is the end of Ethan's carefree existence."

Judy resisted the urge to stick her tongue out at him. She was the adult in the relationship—something she was having trouble remembering today.

Trying to ignore her partner she returned to her wedding commentary. "Mary's reached Ethan, and she's taken his hand. The minister is talking. What a day for WLVH. We've always said Lovehandles was a station where love was more than just a song, but now we've proven it."

"Sentimental hogwash." Peter rolled his eyes.

"They're reciting their vows," she whispered.

"Yeah, Ethan's saying, I promise no more poker with the guys or watching football on Sundays—" He grunted audibly as Judy's elbow hit him firmly in his stomach. "Hey!"

"Shhh." She took a deep breath. Her elbow plowing into his stomach was surprisingly satisfying.

"The minster is announcing Mr. and Mrs. Ethan Westbrook to the guests. Now the two of them are walking back down the aisle together. Oh, you all should see how happy they look."

"Let's wait and see them five years from now when they have a mortgage payment that's too big and a couple kids. Romance tends to fade, and all that's left is two frazzled strangers who stay together for the sake of the kids. We'll see how happy . . . Umph."

"And that's the end of our broadcast. Cassie, who's filling in for Chuck, will be taking your requests this afternoon. Cassie?"

"Thanks Judy. You and Punch have a great time at the reception. Bring me back a piece of cake, would you?"

"Are you going to put it under your pillow, Cass, and dream about me?" Peter broke in.

Cassie laughed. "I might put it under my pillow, but the tradition is you dream about the man you're going to marry. Punch, my love, we both know you're not the marrying kind."

"You've got that right," he said with more enthusiasm than he'd shown the entire wedding broadcast.

"I'll stop by with your cake, Cass."

"Thanks Judy. Have fun. Let's start the hour with 'The Wedding Song' in honor of Ethan and Mary's big day."

Judy tore off her earphones and faced Peter.

"Don't you take anything seriously? Two people finding each other . . . it's amazing; something to be treasured, not mocked."

She gave him a disgusted look, waved at Bill, their technician, and joined the crowd gathering outside the church.

"Maybe you're too invested in Mary and Ethan's wedding."

"We helped bring them together through the contest. And now they've decided to join their lives together. They promised to always be there for each other. What could be more serious than that?"

He rolled his chestnut eyes. "It's an easy promise to make. It's just not such an easy one to keep."

Judy took a step back and glared at him. At five-foot-ten, she met most men eye-to-eye, or even looked down at them, but with Peter she had to crane her head slightly.

Judy had always felt awkward about being taller than most of the men who surrounded her, but with Peter she'd take any edge she could get. "Why do you always do that?"

Momentary confusion filled his dark eyes. "What?"

"Turn everything into a joke."

He chuckled. "Honey, I'm not joking. Look at statistics. Seems to me, a lot of those people who vow to love each other for the rest of their lives either have a very short life span or a very short memory."

"I believe in marriage. And I also believe Ethan and Mary have a great chance of making theirs last for the long haul." She turned her back on him. Sometimes just tuning him out was the easiest way of dealing with Peter's cynicism.

Judy watched the maroon Chevy truck pull away and brushed away a tear. Despite Peter's attitude, the wedding had been every little girl's fantasy. A handsome groom waiting at the end of that long walk down the aisle, his hand extended, his joy written in the smile on his face.

Every little girl wanted to be whisked away by someone who loved her, someone she loved. Every little girl wanted the works—family and friends surrounding her, and love waiting for her at the end of the aisle. A lifetime's worth of love.

Every little girl dreamed about it, but not every little girl got it.

Judy had faced that truth years ago.

Peter waved a hand in front of her face, shaking Judy from the childish daydreams—dreams she thought she'd forgotten years ago.

He looped an arm carelessly over her shoulder. "If you're done getting all goo-goo eyed, it's time to get this show on the road. We need to help Bill pack up."

"There's no hurry." She heard the wistfulness in her own voice. There was no hurry—that had been her motto for years. But recently she'd become aware of the faint ticking of her biological clock, and she began to wonder if she'd ever find someone to love, someone to build a family with.

"Seems there is a hurry. Ted wants us to go to the reception so we can keep the romance alive on next week's show." Peter's tone reflected his displeasure at the prospect.

"Is that a problem for you?" She had planned to attend the reception without their promotion director's prompting. It hadn't occurred to her that Peter wouldn't go.

WLVH had sponsored the "Pickup Lines" contest earlier in the summer. Peter and Judy had covered the couple's two-week stay in a Chevy pickup truck on their early morning radio show. Somewhere along the line, Mary and Ethan stopped feeling like contestants to Judy. They began to feel like old friends.

"I have plans." The look on Peter face said that those plans didn't include attending the reception.

The fact that he had plans wasn't unusual. Peter always had plans, though they rarely included the same woman for more than a week.

Judy turned her attention to the other people in the church's parking lot. As Ethan and Mary pulled away in the maroon Chevy pickup that had brought them together, the crowd began to drift to their various vehicles.

"Why don't you just fill me in Monday morning?" Peter started walking toward the radio station's van.

"What if I have plans?" She followed on his heels.

He turned and rolled his eyes. "Yeah, big ones I imagine."

Judy felt her face flush. Thankfully, his back was to her so he didn't see. The fact that he could embarrass her annoyed her even more than Peter's assumption she had no plans. "What do you mean by that?"

"You know what I mean." He turned and was grinning. "You don't have much of a social life."

"I don't what?"

Her hands seemed to plant themselves on her hips by their own volition.

Judy forced herself to relax and let them drop to her side, but she couldn't help plucking at the hem of her dress.

Peter laughed, and started packing equipment. "Come on Jude, you might as well be a nun for all the dating you do."

"I date." She wanted to push the words from between clenched teeth—her jaws felt brittle enough to break at the slightest touch. Instead, she painted a smile on her face and tried to look as normal as possible.

"When?"

"When what?"

"When is the last time you dated? You talk about everything else on air. I would think we'd all be hearing about all these fantastic men." He looked up from his work and watched her, expectation in his expression.

"Just because some of us don't think our con-
quests should be fodder for the show doesn't mean
we don't have any."

"It doesn't mean you have any either." He must
have sensed trouble, because Peter's manner changed.
"All this dating stuff aside, why don't you go to the
reception and just fill me in? No matter what you say,
we both know you don't have anything better to do."

Judy wanted to deny it, but Peter was right. She
didn't have anything better to do—if by "better" he
meant a date. But she wasn't any more likely to
admit that to him than she was to tell him the her sil-
houette was courtesy of a pushup bra. "If Ted said
we should both go, then I think we should both go."

His pretty boy face scowled. "I told you, I have a
date."

"Well, maybe she'd like to come along." She
smiled again, but this time it was more genuine.
Peter annoyed her often enough, it always felt good
when she could pay him back.

"I don't take women to weddings. It gives them
ideas. Just look at you, all moony and sighing over
the wedding. As if you thought Ethan and Mary were
destined for some romantic happily-ever-after."

"I think they might be." She'd have to be blind not
to see how they looked at each other. That kind of
love meant something. Yes, she really did think they
were a couple destined to make it.

"Ha. Like I said, the statistics don't agree. No, I don't see why you should let your heart get twisted in knots over the wedding. The odds are against them making it work."

Mary was torn between annoyance and amusement. The amusement momentarily won out. That was the thing about Peter, she just couldn't stay mad at him. "You're impossible." She chuckled. "I always thought it was just an act for the show. But I'm beginning to suspect that you are a curmudgeon."

"A what?"

"An old grump who's set in his ways. And your ways are very curmudgeony."

Peter ignored her teasing and asked, "So, are you going to the reception?"

He smiled a smile that had probably melted a thousand women's hearts, using Judy's momentary amusement to his advantage.

"Are you?" she countered.

He shook his head. "Not if I can help it."

"Fine." Amusement faded, replaced by annoyance once again.

That was the other thing about Peter, the amusement never lasted.

"Now don't give me that look. We both know you don't have anything better to do and I do—her name's Belinda."

"Ah, you remember her name this time."

"I always know their names. At least for as long as I'm seeing them." He closed the van's rear door.

"A week shouldn't overly tax your little mind." A week was the longest period she remembered any one woman being in Peter's life.

He ignored her, turned and called, "Hey, Bill. I think I've got this stuff all ready to go in the truck." He started walking toward his car. "My memory is just fine, thank you."

Was that annoyance in his voice? Judy wasn't ready to let go of her momentary advantage; she dogged his heels. "Really? What was the name of the teeny-bopper you dated last month?"

He turned. Judy pulled up short and sucked in a startled breath. She had just avoided running into him. Being so close to Peter always left her a little breathless.

Maybe she was allergic to his cologne?

"She wasn't in her teens." His perfectly straight teeth clenched as he spit out the words.

Judy's teeth surprisingly no longer felt the slightest need to clench; in fact, she managed a pretty genuine smile. "How old was she?"

"Twenty-one."

"Sorry, the *tweeny*-bopper. And, what did you say her name was?"

"Sue?" Peter didn't sound very sure.

Judy's smile broadened into laughter. "Lucy. You called her Lou."

He shoved his hands into his pockets. "I was close."

"But no cigar." She reached over and patted his shoulder. "Now, are you going to the reception?"

"You really won't do it for me?" he asked.

She shook her head. "I really won't."

"I didn't RSVP," he tried.

Judy's smile broadened. "I did for both of us, so you're safe."

"What about Belinda? They're not expecting her." Peter realized he was clutching at straws, but he'd clutch at anything that would get him out of attending the reception. He hated weddings and everything associated with them.

"I'm sure Mary won't care. There's always someone who RSVP's they're coming and then doesn't show."

"Fine," he muttered.

"Fine," she echoed with saccharine sweetness.

It was Judy's sweetness that irked Peter O'Brien the most. She was the type of woman whose rose colored glasses saw all cups as half full.

Peter knew better. Most silver linings were in actuality lead.

He pulled his cell phone out of his jacket pocket and, as he suspected, Belinda didn't bat an eye at the change of plans. He snapped the receiver back in place and thrust the phone in his pocket. He almost wished Belinda would have stood up to him. He'd promised her an evening to do as she wished, but instead he was dragging her along on the job.

She should have been annoyed, should have read him the riot act; instead, she just agreed.

The only woman who ever stood up to him was Judy. At first it had intrigued him, now it just annoyed the hell out of him.

He watched Judy walk toward her car, her backside swaying lazily back and forth as she walked. The silk of her tan dress emphasized her sleek body in a way that begged any red-blooded man to look.

Peter did look, but that's as far as it would ever go with Judy.

She should wear darker, more passionate colors. I'd put her in red. Dark red.

He shook his head. Peter was immune to Judy— her backside and her sunny personality. He found her sweet, wholesome act annoying.

Annoyance. That's what he felt as he watched her silk-covered backside sashay away from him.

Just let her fool the rest of the male population, but she wasn't fooling Peter O'Brien. He knew the truth. Nothing was ever as good as it looked—he took another glance at her figure—no matter how good it appeared.

* * *

"They look so happy," Judy said, more to herself than to Peter and Belinda.

Belinda Carter looked like the type of woman that Judy always pictured Peter dating. Petite, gorgeous, perfect make-up and hair. The only thing that surprised Judy was her intelligence. She was a vice president of a bank but didn't feel the need to advertise her position.

Confidence, looks, and brains.

Judy sighed and took another sip of her wine. It wasn't fair. She knew she wasn't at a loss for brains, though some people—she looked at Peter—might argue the point. No, she was smart enough not to worry about brains. But working with Mr. Peter drop-dead-gorgeous O'Brien was enough to shake any woman's confidence.

Add to that their days started at four in the morning. Judy had decided long ago that it was impossible to be a sex goddess before nine. She'd also decided that God had invented ponytails just for women who worked early.

Today, when she'd looked in the mirror while dressing, she'd felt pretty good about her looks. She wasn't breathtakingly beautiful, but she was more than passable.

She leaned back in the chair and watched the happy couple dancing, Ethan's arms wrapped possessively around the radiant Mary. Mary's flamboyant mother was dressed in an orange dress and was dancing with Ethan's father. She wondered if maybe there was something more than in-law friendliness going on there.

"Look at them," she said to Peter. "Do you think Charles and Gilda . . . well, maybe—" The look in Peter's eye made her stop short and feel foolish.

He turned to Belinda. "Seems our Jude hasn't shaken the touch of romance-itis she caught at the wedding." He sounded pleasant enough, but Judy was aware that he was mocking her.

"I don't blame her. Everything is so beautiful." Belinda smiled kindly at Judy. "Weddings can make any woman's heart turn to romance."

Peter frowned. "Women."

Judy looked at Peter's date again. Belinda Carter was certainly a change of pace for Erie's most eligible bachelor. "I should do some circulating and let the two of you enjoy the romantic atmosphere."

Peter's frown said that he didn't intend to enjoy anything at this wedding.

"Maybe I should join you?" He glanced nervously at Belinda, who was watching the couples on the dance floor.

"No. I can handle this. You just sit and observe the party so you can lend us that ever-so-captivating man's eye view on Monday."

She left the couple feeling a good deal happier.

Peter looked sufficiently miserable, and Belinda looked sufficiently romantic. Yes, her work was done. And she couldn't be happier with the results.

She worked her way across the hall, taking mental notes on the party so she could share it all on Monday's show.

"Your glass is empty," a rich male voice said.

Judy turned. "Pardon?"

She recognized the tuxedoed man whose eyes were slightly less than level with hers, but couldn't place his name.

"I said, your glass is empty." He extended a hand. "Barney Clark, Ethan's friend. And you're Judy Bently from the radio."

Barney's hand was firm and warm as they shook. "Best man, right?"

He looped his arm over her shoulder and steered her toward the bar. "See how quick you are? I've been trying to convince Mary that I was the best man since the get-go, but she only had eyes for Ethan." He shrugged. "Go figure."

Judy allowed him to maneuver her through the crowd and laughed. "Guess one man's steak is another man's dead cow."

Barney thought a moment. "Am I the dead cow or the steak in that particular analogy?"

Judy leaned against the bar and grinned. "I think we'll just leave you the best man."

"Now you're talking." He motioned to the bar-tender who refilled Judy's drink. "Why don't you drink that down and then I'll ask you to dance."

"Why don't you ask me now?" She obligingly took a sip of the sweet red wine.

"Because I've always found my chances improve in direct proportion to the amount of liquor the woman is drinking."

Judy found herself laughing again. "You're saying you need them drunk to stand a chance?"

"I'm saying it doesn't hurt. Especially when you're best friends with someone like Ethan."

Ethan Westbrook was indeed a nice looking man, not as good looking as Punch—but then, who was?

And though Barney wasn't exactly gorgeous, he was cute. There was something in his smile and the way the curls in his dark hair seemed to run amuck that was endearing. Wisely, Judy kept the thought to herself. "You don't need to get me drunk to get a dance, at least you wouldn't if I danced."

"You don't dance?"

"Sure I do . . . like I have a stick up my butt. That's why I avoid dancing in public."

Anxious to talk about anything but her lack of dancing ability, Judy switched back to their earlier subject. "I know what you mean about Ethan, though. I had all these cute, petite little cheerleader-type friends. My nickname in high school was

Beanpole Bently. They even stitched it on my basketball jersey."

Barney leaned close and whispered in her ear. "Honey, if you're how they grow beanpoles these days, I have a new favorite vegetable."

Judy found herself giggling at the absurd compliment.

"Still, I'm afraid all the compliments in the world aren't going to help you get that dance. I'm serious, I won't."

"I'm sure you're not that bad."

Barney was at least three or four inches shorter than she was, and she was sure they'd never fit together comfortably on the dance floor. "You're just going to have to take my word for it, because I'm not about to show you."

"This isn't just a way to blow me off?" Barney eyed her suspiciously.

"No." Judy took his arm. "Why don't you introduce me to the happy couple's friends and family? I know it's not quite a dance, but it gives us both something to do."

"Weddings are hell if you don't have anyone to be miserable with?" Barney asked.

Judy glanced at Peter and Belinda. "Something like that."

Barney's eyes followed the direction of her gaze. "Ah."

"Pardon?"

"Some guys have all the luck," he muttered.

"Luck?"

Barney just smiled and led her toward a table of the happy couple's friends.

Chapter Two

Peter's eyes narrowed as he stared at Judy hanging all over some man she'd just met. She was working the room like some social butterfly—flitting from one person to another.

And he couldn't help but see that other men were noticing how good she looked tonight. The tan silk she was wearing might not be red, but it accented her dark hair, which was finally escaping the bun thing she had shellacked the unruly strands into for the occasion.

Judy's hair had intrigued him from their first day working together. It seemed to live a life of its own, escaping any style she attempted, even breaking free of the stupid ponytails she seemed to favor. Those brown curls had their own agenda.

Sometimes Peter found himself ready to reach out to tuck a stray strand behind her ear. It was only through sheer force of will that he stopped himself each time, but some days it was a near thing.

He watched Judy and the man who held her much too close. Peter knew he was Ethan's best man, but who was he to Judy? Was he the reason Judy had been so hot to come to this party?

"Peter?"

He realized that Belinda had finished . . . what had she been talking about? "Huh?"

"Did you hear a word I said?"

He took a stab in the dark. "You want another drink?"

Belinda steepled her fingers under her chin and studied him thoughtfully. "Why do you bother dating me?"

"Pardon?"

Here it was. The big discussion. Date a woman more than once, and they seemed to take it as a commitment.

Belinda was a nice enough looking woman, at least she was when she wasn't frowning, like she was now. She was smart and fun. But just because he enjoyed her company that didn't mean he wanted to settle down with her. He didn't want to settle down with anyone.

"I mean it, Peter. I'd have to be blind not to notice the way your eyes follow her."

"Her who?"

"Judy." Belinda looked in his partner's direction across the hall. "You haven't taken your eyes off her since she left the table."

Peter forced himself to meet Belinda's gaze. "We're partners, that's all. I was just seeing what she was doing."

He glanced in Judy's direction again, and she was still wearing the guy's arm like a coat. He was going to have to talk to her. That kind of attitude gave a man ideas.

Actually almost any kind of attitude gave a man ideas—he should know. And Peter didn't want this man getting those ideas about Judy.

He'd have to warn her.

Belinda looked in Judy's direction. "You're seething because she's with some man."

Peter decided to ignore Judy's annoying flirting and concentrate on his slightly crazy date. "Why would I care who she was with?"

How had he not noticed that, despite her brains and looks, Belinda was nuts? She thought he was jealous about Judy being with another man? How absurd!

Belinda didn't look crazy as her eyebrows rose and she stared him down. No, she looked every inch the banker ready to foreclose a mortgage. "Now, why you should care who Judy's with is a question you should be asking yourself."

"She's just a co-worker, nothing more."

Judy was his on-air partner. He couldn't even say they were friends. He made it a point to keep business and real-life separate.

"Me thinks thou dost protest too much."

He searched for a comeback. "And I think you're jealous." It was lame and they both knew it, but Belinda didn't have to laugh, he thought bitterly.

God, he hated weddings.

"Honey, we both knew up front what this relationship was about—convenience. Maybe even a sense of loneliness."

It was his turn to laugh. "You say that, but all women—"

"I'm not all women."

Peter really looked at Belinda—really looked at the woman he'd been dating. "No, I don't suppose you are."

"I'd like to think you respect me enough to be honest with me."

He frowned and glanced at Judy again. "Okay, so maybe I think she's attractive, but there are a lot of attractive women in the world . . . yourself included," he added as an afterthought.

"Oh, be still my heart. Compliments like that just turn a girl's head." She laughed, reached across the table and took his hand. "Why don't you just ask her out? Something non-business related."

"Dating people you work with never works out."

Peter had been there, done that, and had absolutely no desire to do it again.

"Okay, so let's not rush into dating. How about dancing? Dancing with people you work with couldn't be too dangerous, could it?"

His eyes narrowed. "Are you trying to dump me?"

She squeezed his hand. "It would serve you right if I did, but I don't think there was enough of a relationship here to dump. Let's just say, we're mutually deciding we're better off as friends than as a couple."

She glanced at Judy and her companion. "And let's just say, if you were to ask Judy to dance I would be enough of a friend to occupy her companion."

"You are a sly and devious woman." There was a hint of admiration in his voice.

"It's a dog-eat-dog world, and I prefer caviar to dogfood." She rose. "So what do you say? Let's go talk to Judy and her friend."

Peter was sure there was some major flaw in Belinda's reasoning, but, for the life of him, he couldn't think of what it was.

Dancing with Judy couldn't hurt a thing. It wasn't as if he was asking her to marry.

No, he was just asking her to dance with him.

One dance.

Peter wasn't going to dance with Judy because he wanted to. He was going to dance with her to save her from the man she was draped all over. He just didn't like the look of the guy. Ethan's best man had shifty eyes. Peter didn't need to be closer to realize that he wasn't right for Judy.

Belinda would certainly be able to handle him, though—she had enough experience with men. But Judy was too innocent for her own good. She'd be eaten alive by the shark.

"Let's go," he said to Belinda. They maneuvered their way through the crowd. Judy was still talking and laughing—and hanging all over—Ethan's best man.

Barney. That was his name.

"Hi, Judy." Belinda flashed one of her thousand-watt smiles at the couple. "Who's your friend?"

"Barney. Barney Clark. This is Peter's date, Belinda—?" She left the name hanging, a question in the air.

"Belinda Carter." She extended her hand. "You're Ethan's best man?" They shook hands for an inordinately long time before they let go.

"I was just trying to convince Judy of that fact."

Belinda didn't move from Barney's side. "The best man, huh? You could try and convince me on the dance floor, if you like."

"You don't mind?" Barney asked Judy over his shoulder even as he moved toward the dance floor.

Judy gave him a gentle push. "Go have fun."

Peter watched his on-air partner closely. Her gaze followed Barney and Belinda.

Was she upset?

"We could dance too, if you like," he offered.

Judy shook her head. "No thanks."

"If you can't dance with lover boy, you won't dance at all?"

"I don't dance." Her gaze was on the dancers, not Peter.

He moved closer and whispered in her ear. "Don't dance at all, or don't dance with me?"

"Are you trying to flirt with me, Punch?" There was confusion in her blue eyes.

Peter couldn't be annoyed that she obviously didn't understand him. He didn't understand himself.

Funny, he'd worked with her a year, but he'd never noticed what an odd shade of blue her eyes were. They were a lake blue, dusky and almost grey.

They were the kind of eyes that could hide secrets. What secrets did Judy have?

She blinked twice and finally answered. "Never mind, that was a stupid question. We don't flirt with each other. Annoy each other maybe, but nothing more. And to answer your question, I don't dance at all. Worried I was snubbing you?"

"I could teach you."

"How to snub more effectively? I'm sure you could."

He sighed. She wasn't going to make this easy. Then again, nothing about Judy Bently had ever been easy. "No. How to dance."

She shook her head. A few more curls broke free

from her careful styling, springing into wild disarray. "I don't think so. Like I was telling Barney, I hold my own on a basketball court, but on a dance floor . . . let's just say it's not a pretty sight."

"Trust me." He led her toward the floor. Not exactly led, pulled her.

It was just one dance, he reminded himself, as he drank in the scent of her, the feel of her. He couldn't have stopped himself now, not for anything. He wasn't sure why, but he needed to hold her in his arms, if only for a dance.

Judy wanted to run and hide as Peter led her toward the floor. She should protest—she really should. But somehow she couldn't seem to find the words, or the willpower to run.

She didn't enjoy being on display, and didn't enjoy making a fool of herself. Both were likely to happen if she stepped on the dance floor and let herself be swept away by Peter O'Brien.

It would be easy to be swept away by Peter. She'd had a bit of a school girl crush on him when they had first started working together last year. She was over that now . . . so over that.

"Peter," she protested, holding herself stiff. She didn't want to touch him. Or rather, she did want to touch him, but that's what made it dangerous.

"Just relax and follow my lead. You don't have to do anything but take small steps, I'll do the rest." He frowned. "Come on, Judy, any fool can turn circles. I wasn't planning to tango."

Peter led her to the middle of the floor and fell into the slow rhythm of the song. His hands wrapped around her waist, but Judy stood stiff, unsure what to do next.

"Wrap your arms around my neck and relax," he whispered in her ear.

She obeyed, though she wasn't sure why she was listening to him. She gingerly laced her arms around his neck. Some women might have problems reaching his neck. But the advantage of being tall was that she didn't have to reach very much at all—they seemed to fit together perfectly.

"This is as relaxed as I get." She tried to maintain some distance.

Peter gave a little tug, pulling her closer. "You're so stiff that one good squeeze and you'd break."

"So don't squeeze."

"Honey, you're too tempting not to."

Suddenly she relaxed. She knew this Peter. Flirting with women came as naturally to him as breathing. It didn't mean anything.

"Well, resist that urge," she scolded, back in her on-air personality mode. "Does that sort of line really work with other women?"

He didn't need to answer . . . she already knew it did. But not with her. Never with her. They were co-workers. Nothing more.

Punch's face was nestled against her neck. It almost felt as if his lips brushed her neck. No, she must have imagined it.

Peter O'Brien wasn't interested in her. He never had been, and he never would be.

"I'm not good at resisting." His breath caressed her neck.

The fluttering of her heart must be from the exertion, it couldn't be from dancing with Peter. "I've noticed."

"You're not going to let yourself enjoy this, are you?" He sighed dramatically.

Judy grinned. She pushed back against him and looked into his dark eyes. "Maybe if you were quiet and stopped your macho-male-stud-muffin display, I could."

"Are you telling me to shut up?"

Thankfully, he'd moved his head off her shoulder so he could see her.

Judy smiled. "In my very polite, lady-like way, yes."

Peter chuckled. "That's what I like about you, Jude. You don't let me get away with anything."

He was quiet after that.

But as much as Judy wanted to relax and quiet her brain, his offhanded comments played in a continuous loop.

He liked her? He couldn't resist? What did he mean by that?

A worse question occurred to her, what did she want him to mean?

Nothing, that's what he meant. He was just a flirt. Nothing more, nothing less.

Nothing. And that's what she wanted him to mean, of course.

Peter was a lady's man and her colleague. On a good day, they could even be called friends. As just a friend and colleague, she shouldn't notice that he smelled good. His cologne was something she'd noticed the first day, and it was something she couldn't help but notice every time she was close to him. He smelled better than any man she'd ever met.

She had dated a guy named Jonathan for over a month last spring. She'd almost asked Peter what cologne he used so she could buy Jonathan some. Things had been rather flat between them, and she'd thought a scent upgrade might increase her interest.

In the end, she couldn't do it. Wanting her boyfriend to smell like her radio partner seemed just a bit too kinky.

Judy realized Peter had been right when he said dancing with him would be painless. She was almost enjoying herself. Pressed against him, drinking in the scent of him, swaying to the romantic music. It was a heavenly mix.

What on earth was that scent?

Judy craned her neck and quietly sniffed his neck.

"Like it?" Peter asked.

She slammed her head back against his shoulder. "What?"

"My neck?"

"I don't know what you're talking about," she mumbled into the soft fabric of his jacket.

He took her chin in his head and tugged until her gaze met his. "Liar. Your head's been moving in that direction for a while."

Heat rushed to her cheeks. "Maybe you have a bony shoulder and I was just looking for a comfortable area."

"Did you find one?"

"No. You're just bony and bumpy all over."

"Shut up, Jude, and dance."

Judy gratefully obeyed and nestled her face back against his shoulder. She didn't plan to make a habit of obeying, though. Peter had enough women blindly following his wants and whims.

The song faded and she pulled away. "Thank you."

Peter let go, and gave her an odd look. "You're welcome." He hesitated a moment. "Listen, Belinda and I have to go. I did my duty and showed up here. Now I'm officially off the clock."

Judy nodded. "You were better behaved than I imagined you could be."

"I'm not sure if that was a compliment or not, but I'll take it as one and say goodnight." He started to walk off the dance floor, then stopped and turned. "See you Monday."

"Yes, Monday."

Peter nodded and walked off the dance floor. Judy slowly followed him off.

He collected his date . . . his date. Belinda was his date, he'd only danced with Judy because he felt he had to, because Barney was dancing with Belinda. They were colleagues, nothing more, nothing less.

Nothing more.

It wouldn't do to forget that.

"It's five-fifteen and sixty-nine degrees on this beautiful Monday morning here in Erie. This is Punch O'Brien—"

"—and Judy Bently. Punch and Judy in the morning here at WLVH Lovehandles, where love is more than just a song."

She nodded her head at Peter. Their silent cues helped keep the dialogue flowing.

The small studio might be claustrophobic to some, but it was a second home to Judy. The panels, the stools, the microphones—they were her bread and butter.

The walls were padded for acoustics, but with Peter around, padded walls were certainly appropriate. When he was in one of his wild moods, he was enough to drive anyone nuts.

He picked up his cue. "Saturday, we broadcasted live from Ethan and Mary Westbrook's wedding." He grimaced.

Judy nudged her mike a little higher. "I know you all remember WLVH's "Pickup Lines" contest at the beginning of the summer. We've been saying for years that Lovehandles is a place where love is more than just a song, but at Ethan and Mary's wedding on Saturday, we finally proved it."

Peter silently gagged for Judy's benefit, then picked up his cue. "And the other thing we proved this summer is our Judy has a deep romantic side. You all should have seen her on Saturday, sighing over every little thing."

Judy made a graphic gesture that summed up her annoyance with her partner. The beauty of radio was she could get away with it.

She pasted a smile on her face. One of the first lessons she'd learned was that the audience could *hear* smiles. "I think we're all aware that Punch isn't known for his romantic side, and that's too bad. I liked his date. Belinda seemed like too nice a lady for our love 'em and leave 'em Punch O'Brien."

Peter's eyes snapped in her direction, but the audience wouldn't be able to detect the slightest hint of his glare.

Judy just smiled sweetly. "Today on Lovehandles, we're looking for your most unusual romantic stories. I mean, Ethan and Mary discovered love while they lived in a brand new Chevy truck. How about all of you?"

Still glaring, but right on cue, Peter said, "Give us a call at seven-three-five-WLVH."

"Now, here's Celine Dion's latest release . . ."

Judy hit two switches on her panel, removed her headphones and turned to Punch, her on-air smile melting into a frown. "Will you get off my case?"

His big brown eyes widened, a portrait of innocence. "What?"

She grabbed a stack of commercial tapes they'd used the last hour and started putting them back into their slots in the racks. She'd found talking to him was easier if she avoided eye contact. "I'm not a romantic. It was a nice wedding, that's all. End of story."

"Yeah, that's why you got all moony-eyed over the whole thing." He batted his eyes for effect and held his hands to his chest in a Southern belle imitation.

"I did not." Judy shoved the tape into its slot with more force than necessary. Better to shove a tape than a colleague, she thought. Though shoving Peter O'Brien would have its advantages.

His fingers drummed the tape machine. "I refuse to behave like a child and say 'did too,' but you know you did."

"I simply appreciate that somewhere in the midst of the contest, Ethan and Mary became friends and fell in love. Love is precious and deserves to be celebrated when it's found. Plus, I had a great time with Ethan's friend, Barney."

"How good a time?" His fingers picked up tempo.

Judy grabbed a stack of CDs they'd played and began returning them to their slots as well. "Oh, probably about as good a time as you had with Belinda."

His fingers stopped dead mid-strum. "See, the wedding made you so moony-eyed that even that Barney looked good. You know, you tower over him."

Beanpole Bently tried to ignore the barb's direct hit. Her voice was soft as she said, "Barney does look good. He's also intelligent and funny—so of course I had a good time. And I might have to physically look down at him, but I can look up to the person he is." Her eyes met his. "You know, frequently it's the other way around."

She could see her words penetrated Peter's thick head, but she wasn't sure if she felt vindicated or not.

It was Peter who broke their gaze. "Fine. You do what you have to."

"I was planning on it." Top on her must-do list was forgetting how it felt to dance with Peter, as a matter of fact.

"Are we going to take any of those calls, or are you just going to nag all morning?" He nodded at the blinking phone lines.

Judy consulted the log and pulled the last couple CDs for the next hour. "You're just sitting there. Feel free to take one."

Peter shifted in his seat and pressed a line. "WLVH, Lovehandles."

"Hi, Punch."

"Hi. Did you call with a story for us? Something to melt Judy's romantic heart?" Peter asked the woman.

"Yes."

Judy put down a stack of tapes and leaned over her microphone. "What's your name?"

"Oh, I'm sorry, I'm Sherry."

Punch motioned at the board. "Hey, Sherry, can you hold on a minute?"

"Sure."

Judy flipped a switch. "That was Celine Dion and here's James Taylor," she said into the mike.

They had four minutes and thirty seconds until they were back on the air. She hit the record button on the tape machine. They could tape phone conversations and edit them before they put them on the air. It was the best way to make sure nothing inappropriate went out over the airwaves.

"Okay, Sherry, what's your unusual romantic story?"

"I met my fiancé in jail."

"That's unusual? Why, I've met some of my favorite women in prison." Punch chuckled. His rich throaty laughter was a trademark on the morning show. "Did he have a big tattoo? Most of my prison women did."

"No, sorry, no tattoo. You see, he's the prison pharmacist. I work there as a nurse and—"

Judy leaned over her mike and interrupted. "So neither of you were actually incarcerated?"

"No. But, Carl, that's my fiancé, likes to tell everyone we met in jail. He wanted our wedding cake shaped like a jail cell."

"Well, some of us might consider marriage very similar to jail. Too bad about the tattoo though," Punch mused.

His anti-marriage prattle was getting to her, and she wasn't sure why. Part of their on-air shtick was taking opposite ends of most debates. Listeners loved their on-air spats. For a year, that relationship had worked wonderfully, but lately something had changed and Judy didn't know what it was or what to do about it. His constant harping on marriage being worse than prison, his string of girlfriends . . . all of it was annoying her.

She forced herself to concentrate on the caller. "When's the wedding?"

"Next week. You know, I thought I had a pretty good story for you. But Punch's stories sound like they might be better." Sherry's laughter filled the studio.

"But the management frowns on him sharing too many of them. We run a G-rated program. And, I loved your story."

"Thanks. Before I let you both get back to work I

just wanted to tell you how much I enjoyed your broadcast of the wedding on Saturday."

"I'll be sure to pass it on to the management. Give us a call after your wedding and let us know how the jail cell cake goes over." Judy held back a sigh. Maybe Peter was right, maybe she was a closet romantic.

"I'll do that," their caller promised. "I'll even save you a piece, Judy. You know they say if you put a slice of wedding cake under your pillow you'll dream about who you're going to marry."

"Dreaming about your white knight, Judy?" Peter rejoined the conversation with all the grace of a brick.

"No," she said simply, not adding that she'd about given up any hopes of finding a knight for herself. It wasn't in the cards.

She glanced at Peter O'Brien, then said into the mike, "No, I've given up on dreaming about white knights and other such fairytales."

Chapter Three

Judy studied Peter. No, there were no white knights on her horizon.

"I don't think I'll ever marry," she told their prison nurse caller. "Working with Punch five days a week is as much of a commitment as I want to make. Speaking of commitments, working with Punch could easily lead to one for me. A commitment to bedlam. You can visit me at the asylum and slip me a piece of that cake."

"You've got it. I'll have my Dad drop it off next Monday. He works out in your neck of the woods."

"That would be great. Thanks for calling."

Punch jabbed the button that disconnected the line. "We'd better take another call. There was nothing useable there."

"I'm just going to edit the part about bringing us some cake, and I think we've got a great piece."

"You do whatever you want to. You always do." Peter's voice was unusually sharp.

Judy glanced up. "What do you mean by that?"

He scowled and shrugged.

"Okay, then. We've got twenty seconds. You lead in with the time and the "what was your most unusual romantic story" bit to lead into the tape. There's less than a minute's worth."

"Fine." Monosyllabic. That wasn't like Peter.

Judy studied him as he chatted into the mike. What was wrong? She couldn't think of anything she'd done to upset him. She tried to put her worries out of her mind.

Hours later, as their show wound down, Peter was still acting odd—odd being a relative term.

She had, however, decided what was wrong with her. Her life was nuts, and so was she. She was sitting at a meeting with the promotion and program directors, sure that any last threads of sanity were unraveling.

"That's absurd," she said again. Her protests made no difference, but she continued making them any way.

Ted Hyatt, WLVH's promotion director, ignored her completely, his blond head bent over papers, exposing its bare center to the other three members of the meeting.

Stu Stewartson, the station's program director, didn't ignore her. He merely sent her one of his more patronizing smiles.

Ted's newest idea didn't appear to bother Peter at all. Whatever was bothering him wasn't the meeting they were sitting in.

The morning show had gone smoothly, their on-air banter unaffected by his mood. She didn't have a name for it. He wasn't angry . . . maybe pensive was a good word. But whatever he was, he wasn't saying much to her, or to Stu and Ted either, for that matter.

"Here." Ted thrust a sheet of paper at her. "Look at that jump."

Judy stared at the figures. "So, ratings went up during the contest, and then during Ethan and Mary's wedding." She passed the paper to Peter, who glanced at it and then passed it to Stu.

"What I'm saying is people seem to really love Punch and Judy going out into the public. If that's what people want, that's what they'll get."

"But the zoo?" The fact that her life was a zoo was no secret, but that didn't mean she wanted to air the fact to the world.

"It's just one show."

"Peter?" she asked, hoping for some help.

"Whatever. It's just a job. I don't imagine it matters where we do it." He'd gone from pensive to apathetic.

"But a zoo?" Judy pressed.

She liked the zoo and enjoyed the animals. But she

didn't think she wanted to be put on exhibit too. She liked being anonymous at the studio.

"Listen, this is just the first of many public appearances I've been setting up, and it's for a good cause. We'll be raising money for the new exhibit." Ted's voice was tight, his patience obviously thin.

"And are all the public appearances going to be so glamorous?" Judy asked.

Men. The entire species was exasperating.

"We're still doing that 'Presque Isle Splash Bash' at the peninsula at the end of the summer. Is that glamorous enough for you?" Stu's fingers tapped his annoyance against the table top.

"As long as you don't expect me to wear a bathing suit. I guess it's glamorous enough. After being put in a cage at the zoo, just about anything looks good."

Ted nodded absently. "Fine, then it's settled. Punch and Judy will be at the zoo next week, then there's that 'Gelatin Challenge' that weekend, and the 'Bash' the week after that. We'll start really promoting Punch and Judy on the town."

"You truly think Erie wants to see us in a cage, doused in gelatin, and in swimwear?" Judy had her doubts, especially about the swimsuit part.

"I'm not sure they want to see Punch in swimwear, but I don't think anyone would mind seeing you." Ted had been hitting on Judy for the entire year she'd worked at WLVH, and for the entire year, she'd been dodging his attempts.

Images of Peter in a small Speedo swimsuit flitted through Judy's mind. She might not be interested in him, but she couldn't deny that looking at him was a pleasure. And she imagined looking at him in a Speedo would be even more pleasurable.

She ignored the internal picture and tried to concentrate on the meeting. "If I agree to suffer all these indignities, do you suppose you could try to set up one, just one, semi-classy thing?"

"Let me see what we can do."

"See what I can do," she mumbled as she stormed from the office and into the hall. "I'd like to show Ted what I can do. And, what about Stu? You'd think he'd step in and say something."

"What did you want him to say?" Peter trailed behind her, his long legs easily keeping up with her furious pace.

"Something, anything. You could have as well." She pushed the door and walked into the warm summer air and took a deep breath, trying to calm herself.

Punch seemed calm enough for both of them. "Listen, I learned a long time ago there's no fighting with promotion directors. They have statistics for hearts and dollar signs for souls."

"And no sense of taste," she muttered, walking toward her Jeep.

"What do you mean?"

"That whole beach thing. I don't like the idea of them parading me around in a bathing suit."

The zoo and the gelatin made more sense to Judy than Ted's comment on her in a bathing suit. She bore a definite resemblance to Popeye's girlfriend when she wore one—all straight lines, not a curve in sight.

"Why do you always do that?" Peter's voice was sharp again.

"What?" She glanced up at the man. He'd been confusing her all morning. Actually, it had started Saturday at the wedding. Maybe Peter had been right—weddings made people goofy.

"Why do you insist on talking as if you just crawled out from under some rock? You've got a shape women would kill to have."

Judy glanced down, and without Saturday's push-up bra, she saw her toes. She wasn't sure that was what most women wanted to see, or most men, either.

"Most women want to look like a ruler, straight as a board?"

"When's the last time you looked at yourself? Really looked?"

"There comes a day when you look in the mirror and know you'll never grow up and be the beautiful fairytale princess. It's a day you know that this is it— as good as it gets. That's the day you grow up and face reality."

"Maybe you don't see what's really in the mirror. Maybe a wicked queen cast a spell on your fairytale mirror, hiding what's really there."

Judy snorted.

"Hey, if you can toss fairytales around, then so can I."

"Why would a wicked queen care what I thought?"

"Because," he said softly, moving closer, "if you saw what was truly there in that mirror—what the rest of the world saw when they looked at you— you'd be dangerous. Because if you knew deep down in your gut how truly beautiful you were, no one—no wicked queen, no prince, no ordinary man—could stand against you."

Her breath caught and she felt her heartbeat quicken, one after another.

For a moment, for one brief, fleeting second, Peter moved in and she thought he was going to kiss her. He was standing so close that if she moved even a little, they'd be touching.

But suddenly he pulled back and, with that little bit of distance, Judy was able to breathe and think again.

She snorted. "Lay off the lines, O'Brien. I'm not one of your ladies. I'm not someone that you have to try and shmooze. I know what I am, and I'm comfortable with it."

His hands were clenched at his side. "I don't think you have a clue."

She snorted again and tugged at her t-shirt.

T-shirts, sweatpants and ponytails.

Every man's fantasy woman, at least that's what Peter was trying to tell her.

Beanpole Bently knew better.

"Well, this Cinderella is heading home for a nap. It's going to be nuts tonight." She fished the keys out of her sweatpants' pockets.

"What's up?"

There was something in his voice that sounded suspiciously like interest.

She studied him a long moment. "Just who are you? A few minutes ago it sounded like you were complimenting me, maybe even trying to comfort me. And now you actually sound like you're interested in my plans."

She shook her head dramatically, sending a dozen tiny curls winging from her ponytail. "Just what have you done with the real Peter O'Brien?"

"Forget it." Peter stalked off toward his Jeep.

Judy hadn't meant to offend him. Peter seemed to thrive on zingers. Something had changed—just what she wasn't sure. But their relationship had altered at the wedding, and it was just growing weirder and weirder.

She jogged after Peter. "Really, it's no big deal. My team has a game at St. Bart's at seven."

"Team?" He slowed his pace.

Judy matched her strides to his, and grinned at his confusion. "Now, there's the Punch I know and love—totally self-absorbed. I told you last month during the show that I'd started coaching a girl's summer league basketball team. Remember?"

He shrugged. "Okay, well, good luck."

Judy stopped and watched him finish crossing the small parking lot to his car. Maybe he'd broken up with Belinda and that was causing this odd mood. She'd liked Belinda, though she didn't think she was right for Peter.

Just what kind of woman did Peter O'Brien need? Now there was a question.

Well, not Belinda, or Mitzy, or any of the other dozen women he'd dated in recent memory. A mental image formed in Judy's head, and she immediately blocked it.

She couldn't waste time thinking about Peter and what he needed in a woman. She had a basketball team to think about.

She turned around and got into her Chevy Lumina. Home to a nap, that's what she needed.

What she didn't need was more weird thoughts about Peter O'Brien.

"These other girls aren't beating us, we're beating ourselves." Judy blew a stray curl off her face in frustration.

"Those aren't girls, they're giants," Jess Jacobs muttered.

Trying to think of something wise—something coach-like—to say was tough. Judy suddenly felt a wave of sympathy for all the coaches she'd alternately loved and hated during her school basketball career.

"It's not size that matters, it's how big your heart is, and how much you want the win. Now, how much do we want the win?"

Muted cheers were the team's response.

Judy resisted the urge to sigh and instead repeated, "How much do we want the win?"

This time the cheers were a little louder.

"Come on, Babes, we've got the heart. We've got the desire. Now all we have to do is get the ball."

Ten seventh and eighth grade girls shouted. "Well, there you go. The three Kates, Abbey, Mandy. You're up the first half of the quarter. Jess, Misty, Sarah, Amanda and Claire, you're in the second part of the quarter. Come on, huddle."

Eleven heads bowed as eleven hands were thrust into the center of the circle. "Bayside Babes rock!" the team screamed.

Five girls ran onto the floor and five more joined Judy on the bench. "Okay, girls, let's run some D!"

Judy watched the game intently, yelling out encouragement and instructions in turn. She ran her team by the *SEA* method of coaching. *State, explain and, affirm.* And sometimes, like today, a few well placed prayers didn't hurt either.

"Watch those picks!"

* * *

Judy was oblivious to everything but the game and the girls.

Oblivious to Peter, who was sitting behind her by a group of doting mothers. The women intermittently cheered for their girls and gossiped.

He had no idea why he was here. He should be out with Belinda. But after the wedding, Belinda had stood by her decision. They were better friends than significant others.

He knew how it would go. He'd been the one to pull back often enough. They'd make the occasional phone call, and maybe even a lunch once or twice, and then they'd maybe see each other out on the town and exchange quick hugs and small talk.

It was too bad. He liked Belinda. She was an intelligent woman. A woman who didn't need all the pretty words and flowery romance that other women seemed to expect. Or, at least that's what he'd thought until Saturday.

Now he wasn't sure.

It was that stupid wedding reception. He had known better than to take a woman anywhere near anything wedding-ish. It gave them ideas—ideas he'd rather they avoided.

His dateless condition was Judy's fault. Now he was at loose ends, condemned to sit at some kids' basketball game in a gym that must be at least ninety degrees, listening to a bunch of women talk about husbands and kids—laughing and moaning in turn—

while a bunch of adolescents totally slaughtered his favorite sport.

Yeah, it was all Judy's fault.

"My husband's cousin, Bert, was here last week, and he liked what he saw," one of the mothers said.

"What's not to like?" another asked.

The first woman nodded her head, greying brown hair flopping. "That's what I said to Hank. It took some doing, but he finally agreed. I'm asking her to an informal barbecue tomorrow night. Bert will be there."

Peter wasn't sure who he felt worse for, the hen-pecked Hank, the soon-to-be-set-up Bert, or whoever the woman was who was going to find herself having dinner with all of them.

"Well, Judy—"

Judy? Punch resisted the urge to run down the bleachers and warn Judy of her fate.

"—needs someone. That job at the radio with that arrogant jerk she works with . . . a woman needs more. Someone like Bert might be just the ticket. Lord knows, he's cute enough."

"Great butt," a large red-head said.

The greying brunette laughed. "He works for a lawn service. All that lawnmowing keeps him in good shape."

"He . . ."

Peter's attention shifted from the conversation to images of Bert and Judy. His Judy.

No, not that she was *his*, but she was his partner. It was up to him to look out for her. And, looking out for her meant keeping her out of the clutches of these match-making mothers.

"Nice lay-up, Kate," Judy shouted.

Peter ignored the women and concentrated on Judy and the game. She was great with the kids, no red-faced screaming or cursing. She praised their successes, and tried to offer suggestions for their weaknesses—and these girls certainly had enough weaknesses.

They were running a zone defense. What they needed to do was run a man-to-man, or in this case, girl-to-girl.

If only Judy had asked him for help, he could have told her as much. But she hadn't said a word.

Okay, maybe she'd said a word at work. But half the time he didn't remember what they bantered about each day on the airwaves. That was work, and he kept his job separate from his personal life. He put in his shift, and then he promptly left his job where it belonged—at the station.

He had to hand it to Judy, though. She was doing a great job with the kids. They'd been down by seven at half-time, and as the third quarter drew to an end, they were only two points behind—just one basket.

Just as he finished the thought, the smallest girl on the team, number ten, took a shot from behind the three point line. *She'll never make it.* But he'd barely finished the thought when the ball sank neatly through the net. As the buzzer screamed, the girl's teammates ran over to her and hugged her.

Judy called the entire team to the bench and talked with them quietly. She huddled the girls around her and talked. He could tell that she was praising them by the smiles that lit the girls' faces, by the way Judy reached out and touched a shoulder here, a strand of hair there.

She stood and sent half the team back out. No playing favorites here, no playing the best. Judy Bently was dividing her team, and the quarter, down the middle.

As she stood, watching the girls take their places, Peter couldn't help but notice how nicely Judy's jeans hugged her slim hips. She didn't think she had a good body—that much was obvious this afternoon when she'd scoffed about anyone wanting to see her in a bathing suit. But Peter wouldn't mind seeing her in one.

He watched her yanking her ponytailed curls tighter into their confinement and admitted to himself that he wanted to see those chestnut curls spilling over him as Jude leaned over him, closer, closer . . .

"Who are you with?" Hank's wife asked.

Peter might have resented her interrupting his fantasies if a particular answer hadn't popped into his head and then right out his mouth. "Judy."

"Judy? Does she play for the Presque Isle Panthers?"

Peter grinned, enjoying himself more than he'd imagined he ever could at a grade school basketball game. "Judy Bently. The Bayside Babes' coach."

"Oh," the woman said, a faint look of bemusement on her face that cleared after a couple moments. "Oh."

Peter smiled, a smile he saved for charming the most difficult of women. "I couldn't help but over-hear you earlier, but since we're talking now, I should mention that I'm afraid Judy isn't in the market for poor Bert's tight butt. You see, she's rather fond of mine."

The woman smiled broadly. "I can see why."

After chatting with her and her cronies a few more moments, Peter broke off, giving the impression that he was watching the game.

In reality, he was thinking about Bert's tight butt and his own. He'd lied when he'd said Judy was fond of it. She appeared totally immune to his butt, and all his other body parts as well.

He was sure it wasn't his body's fault. Enough women chased him for it; so much so, that he found it rather tiresome.

That's one of the reasons he'd liked Belinda. She saw him as more than just a body or some accessory for a woman to occasionally wear. But in a totally uncharacteristic bit of unreasonableness, the fact that Judy didn't seem to notice his attributes was annoying.

He had set the ground rules last year. He didn't mix business with pleasure. Lately, however, he'd begun to suspect that Judy would be a real pleasure.

What was he doing, sitting here, mooning over a woman he worked with? He'd tried an office relationship once, and it had been disastrous. After that, he'd made it a strict policy to never mix the two. Until now, he'd never been tempted to break that rule.

He realized he wasn't here because he was dateless. He was here because he wanted to be. Judy Bently challenged him. She called him on the carpet. She made him laugh. He'd known all that, of course. But after seeing her with that Barney guy at the wedding, he realized that there was more to what he felt for Judy than just business. He wasn't sure just what, but he wanted to find out.

Maybe it was time to break the never mixing dating and business rule? No. He couldn't. He'd made the rule for a reason. But, though he'd known it a second ago, he couldn't exactly remember what that reason was now.

The buzzer sounded the end of the game, and Peter glanced at the scoreboard. Thirty-six, thirty-four. The Bayside Babes had won.

He found himself standing with the rest of the Bayside bleacher, clapping and screaming. The girls walked in a line, shaking the other team's hands.

Judy tagged at the rear of the line, doing the same. Her position exposed her backside. He seemed to have butts on the brain. Hank's wife's mention of Bert's had prompted Peter to check out Judy's. He had to admit, Jude had a pretty fine one. Pert and tight. He'd like to—

Peter cut off the mental images. He was surrounded by women and children. It wasn't the time or place for fantasies about his colleague. He wasn't sure there was a good time or place, but here and now certainly wasn't.

He was ready to make his break when Hank's wife grabbed his elbow. "You just come stand with us and wait for Judy, Mister . . . ?"

By the strength of the woman's grasp, Peter knew resistance was futile. Bowing to the inevitable, he answered, "Peter, Peter O'Brien."

"Peter 'Punch' O'Brien? Judy's partner?"

He nodded, wondering how he'd got himself in such a tremendous mess.

The woman smiled speculatively. "Now, if that isn't a pretty kettle of fish! The two of you an item, and so quiet about it. It was that 'Pickup Lines' contest, wasn't it? Once the love bug starts biting, there's just no stopping it." She turned to the group of women she'd been sitting with. "Girls," this is Punch O'Brien, Judy's partner."

"Oh," came the knowing responses.

"Really, ladies, I have to go."

"Now, now, we don't bite . . . often," said the ring-leader. "You can't just leave without saying something to Judy and to the girls. They'll be so thrilled you came. Maybe you'll mention them tomorrow on your show? Judy's been hesitant to. She said it would be sort of nepotism if she said too much. But if you did—"

"Maybe." He was reluctant to promise this woman anything.

"Now, why don't you tell me—"

The locker room door opened. He was saved from telling her anything. The girls filed out with Judy on their heels.

"Peter?" she said when she spotted him. Questions voiced themselves in those lake blue eyes, but she only voiced one. "What are you doing here?"

The truth of it was, Peter couldn't think of a single, solitary answer to give her.

Unfortunately, Hank's wife didn't have the same problem. "Why, Judy, you don't have to pretend around us. We'd all have to be blind not to see the way Punch here couldn't take his eyes off you the whole game. I think it's sweet."

"Punch and Judy are dating?" one of the girls asked.

A gaggle of mother heads nodded in unison, and Peter knew he'd made a huge, strategical mistake in a war he hadn't known he was campaigning.

* * *

"Are you ever going to talk to me again?" Peter asked the next morning.

Judy took her earphones off, and placed them on the counter. She turned and silently glared at him.

"Jude, you can't ignore me. We work together. Talking is what we do." He flashed his charming smile, the one that had probably saved him from countless women's scorn.

The one that set her teeth on edge.

This was one scornful woman it wouldn't charm. No, a dazzling smile wouldn't save him this time, Judy was firm on that.

"I'm too adult to ignore you. I'm just choosing to save my choice sections of dialogue for after the show." She consulted the music log. It was easier to look at a paper than at him.

"I said I was sorry." He sounded more disgruntled than apologetic.

She looked him in the eye—those marvelously brown eyes that begged to be stared into. Well, she was just going to ignore the begging and focus on anything else.

"Just what are you sorry for, Peter?"

The smile faded, and he had enough sense to look nervous. "For whatever you're mad at me for?"

"Well, that really narrows the list." She consulted the log, and began pulling the next hour's music.

He grabbed her elbow. "Come on, all I did was show up at a game you were coaching."

Judy slammed a small pile jewel cases on the counter. "And you proceeded to tell my team's parents we were dating."

"I didn't quite put it that way." Peter reached for his thermos and poured some coffee into his mug. He mumbled a frustrated oath as it sloshed onto the counter.

"So, how did you put it?"

He slammed the top back on the thermos. Dark eyes snapped as they stared into her own.

"Actually, if you think about it, you owe me."

"Owe you?" She shuffled the cases for something to do with her hands. It was either that, or try to knock some sense into Peter's thick head. She looked at that dark hair that covered his impossibly thick skull, and decided it would take more knocking than she could possibly achieve in one beating.

"That one mom, Hank's wife, was planning to fix you up with some loser cousin . . ." he trailed off and grinned, and when Judy maintained her scowl, he added, ". . . or something."

"You saved me?" She glanced at the clock. "Ten seconds." She put her headset on. "It's seven forty-three here at WLVH." She jerked her hand in Peter's direction.

"It's already seventy-four degrees here at the station, and it looks like it's going to be a scorcher." He looked meaningfully at Judy. "Yes, it's awfully hot."

"And it looks like it might get hotter yet before

things are done." She was going to roast his scrawny butt over the coals.

Okay, so his butt wasn't all that scrawny—it could even be called a fine looking butt. Not that she was calling it that. Not that she was even looking at it.

Well, maybe on occasion she caught a glimpse, but it wasn't as if she actively stared at it—at least not when Peter might notice.

There was a second of dead air space before Peter grabbed the music log and said, "Speaking of hot, here's John Mayer."

Judy jabbed the buttons and tossed her headset down. "Saved me from what?" She picked up the conversation where they had left off.

Peter tossed the music log back on the counter, and faced her glare head on. "From a horrible blind date."

"Did it ever occur to you that it didn't necessarily have to be horrible?" She said the words, but she didn't really believe them. Judy had gone on her share of blind dates and wasn't exactly anxious to go on another. Not that she was going to tell Peter that.

The studio was silent. Both of them had seemingly run out of words—a rare occurrence for radio disc jockeys. What was going on between them?

Judy had been trying to figure it out, but wasn't

any closer to an answer. For an entire year they'd gotten along just fine, and now, suddenly, they were constantly at each other's throats.

Peter broke the silence. "Blind dates by their very definition are horrible."

He took a huge gulp of that horrid, muddy brew he called coffee.

Judy's stomach felt sympathy pains on his behalf.

"You could say Ethan and Mary were set up on the ultimate blind date in the pickup, and that turned out just fine."

He snorted. "A fluke. No one really set them up. It was just dumb blind luck they met in the truck."

"And how do you know that Lady Luck wasn't setting up that date you 'saved' me from?"

"Well, then I'm sorry—"

She cut him off. "We're on in twenty seconds."

Peter picked up his earphones and adjusted his mike. Judy waved at him and he came in on cue. "This is Punch . . ."

"And Judy here at WLVH Lovehandles, where love is more than just a song."

"It's seven forty-eight on a hot end-of-summer Erie morning."

"And, speaking of hot, this morning we want to hear about blind date success stories. Punch and I were just discussing Ethan and Mary, the winners of our Lovehandle's 'Pickup Lines' contest, and the winners of nuptial bliss. Talk about your ultimate blind date success story! So, why don't you tell us yours this morning?"

Peter shot her a dirty look. "While you're thinking, here's Jewel."

Judy turned off the mikes and smiled at Peter. "Great idea, huh? I mean, let's see if your theory of blind dates never paying off is sound."

Peter tossed his earphones on the counter, planted his hands on either side of them, and rose. He leaned across the counter until his face was right next to hers. "What on earth has come over you? You haven't been yourself since the wedding."

Not giving an inch, Judy rose and met his glare with her own. "And how exactly would you define me prior to the wedding?"

"Nice. Comfortable."

"And I'm no longer nice and comfortable?" Maybe she should have taken it as an insult, but Judy just couldn't. She was flustering the unflusterable Peter O'Brien. It was a sight to behold. Suddenly, her anger evaporated.

"You're turning into a . . . well, a woman."

"Honey, you ain't seen anything yet. And, speaking of being yourself, you haven't exactly been the Punch O'Brien I'm used to."

She sank back into her seat and punched a button that connected one of the flashing phone lines, then punched the record button, just in case it was a use-able call. "WLVH, Lovehandles?"

"Hi, Judy this is Ronnie." A sigh drifted over the line and filled the studio. "I've never called a radio station like this."

"Well, we're glad you did, Ronnie. Are you calling with a blind date story?"

"Yes. I met my husband, Bob, on a blind date—a blind date I was set on sabotaging. You see, my brother, Gary, kept setting me up with the biggest batch of loosers imaginable and . . . you see, I decid-ed to get even. So I padded everything paddable, and then I put on my best bimbette performance." The words tumbled over each other, as if it were a race which would get out first.

Judy was laughing. "How good was your best performance?"

There was an answering laugh that floated over the line. "Let's just say, I've decided if I ever give up on computers, I have my next career all lined up."

"Let's get back to the padding. How padded were you?" Punch asked. The leer in his voice matched the one that sparkled in his chestnut eyes.

"Honey, if I sent you a picture I'd ruin you for other women."

"Wow," he exclaimed appreciatively.

"Wow's right. Anyway, somehow Bob figured out what was going on, and after the disastrous blind date ended, he followed me home, and our second anniversary is next week."

Judy raised her eyebrows at Peter and grinned. "I just love happily-ever-afters . . ."

Chapter Four

Peter watched Judy collect her things. She traveled lighter than any woman he'd ever known. Today she had her car keys and sunglasses.

She didn't seem mad anymore, although he wasn't sure why she was mad in the first place. She should have appreciated his saving her from a hellish blind date.

He risked setting her off again by asking, "Are we going to talk now?"

She perched her glasses on top of her head and stuffed the keys in her pocket. Today she had on cut off jeans and a t-shirt. The shorts showed off her mile long legs to perfection, a fact Peter couldn't help but notice throughout their long, antagonistic radio show.

"Do you really want to risk it? I mean, it might get personal, feelings might be discussed. This kind of thing can be messy work, Peter."

"Listen—"

She folded her arms across her chest and took a step forward. "No, you listen—"

Judy was interrupted by the studio door opening. "Hey, how's it going?"

Peter smiled at the elfish woman who entered the room. She was wearing tattered jeans, a denim shirt and a baseball cap over her short blond hair.

"Isn't this your bedtime?" he asked Cassie Grant, WLVH's nighttime DJ.

Cassie yawned. "Dave is sick, or something, and Stu called and begged me to come in. Seems you two are pulling some extra duty this week, and he didn't want to ask."

Peter nodded toward Judy. "He's afraid of Jude here. She's in a snit about our zoo thing."

She was in a snit about more than that, but Peter decided it wasn't wise to mention it.

"Are you going to be able to stay awake for the whole show?" Judy asked.

Cassie nodded. "If they pump enough coffee into me."

"Want me to get you a cup?" Peter asked.

Cassie grinned. "I'd throw myself at your feet, and worship you, but you're used to that kind of thing, so it would be old hat, and goodness knows I hate running with the pack. So, I'll just say thanks."

He walked from the room. As he crossed the hall he realized he'd made a strategical error. Any man knew that leaving two women together when one was disgruntled was bound to be disastrous for the man.

As he reentered the room, coffee in hand, he could see the results of his folly for himself. Both women looked up and Cassie's face was no longer smiling. She took the coffee and offered a terse, "Thank you."

Peter grabbed Judy's elbow. "Jude, we were going to have that meeting now, remember?"

"Are you sure you want to?" Her voice dripped saccharin sweetness.

"Come on." He took her elbow and pulled her to the door. "Have a good one, Cass."

He didn't wait for Cassie's reply, just kept pulling Judy until they'd reached the picnic table in back of the studio. "Talk."

She shook her arm free of his grip, and sat on the picnic table itself, using the seat as a footrest. "Why don't you start?"

She was smiling again and Peter didn't like it—not one bit. Peter had watched enough wildlife shows to realize she had the look of some type of predator ready to jump its prey. Well, Peter Angus O'Brien wasn't anyone's chew toy.

He put on his most anti-prey attitude. "Listen, I'm

not the one who's been walking around here with a chip on my shoulder. You want to vent, you want to get it all off your chest, so talk."

"I can't believe you had the audacity to come to the game last night and tell people we were dating."

He sat next to her. "Like I said, I was just trying to save you from a blind date. I avoid those things like the plague, and I didn't think you'd enjoy them either."

"Peter, you avoid everything that even whiffs of human contact like the plague."

"I date."

She slid further down the table, putting distance between them. It annoyed him, just like everything about her had set his teeth on edge since the wedding. Weddings were occasions designed to torture unmarried men.

"That's just it. You don't have relationships, you just take a woman out until it gets sticky, and then you move on."

"Who needs the trouble?"

"Most people do. You meet someone, and when it gets sticky, you try and work it out because it's worth it."

"Maybe I never found anyone worth the effort." He slid closer to her end of the table.

"Or maybe you're just afraid to let anyone get too close. It's been a year, Peter. We've worked together five, or more, days a week. We talk on the air about everything, and yet, there's no real connection. This is just a job. Now, that's fine. I didn't expect us to become best friends, but I would expect, after a year, that you'd know just a bit about me."

"I know things."

Of course he knew things about Judy. Why would she think he didn't? Maybe he'd forgotten about the basketball team, but that didn't mean he didn't know anything.

"How many siblings do I have?" she asked.

"What?"

Slower, as if he were hard of hearing, she repeated, "How many, and what genders?"

"We've never talked about—"

"Have too."

"Two? One of each."

She started laughing, but there wasn't any joy in the sound. "None."

"That was a trick question." Just like a woman to toss a question you couldn't answer right. Sneaky.

"None, one, ten—doesn't matter. It simply proves that you don't listen."

"How many do I have? You have no idea, right?" He smiled, sure he'd won a point.

"You have one brother, ten years younger, a senior at MIT. His name is Mark, and he's dating a girl named Jill. Your father and mother divorced when you were eight, and you rarely hear from your dad. Your mom remarried right away. You found it tough to like your step-father, though he's a nice enough man. When Mark came along, you found even more reasons to distance yourself from your family."

"Been reading psych books again, Jude?" She was infuriating when she was right. Worse than that, she was sexy as hell.

"I'm right." She crossed her arms across her chest and got that stubborn look.

That look should have sent him running in another direction, any direction. Instead, Peter had the insane desire to wrap his arms around her and kiss the stubborn look away. He tried to block the image from his mind. It was time for a strategic retreat—a hasty one.

He cleared his throat. "Listen, you've made your point. I don't like you interfering, and making assumptions about my life. I won't make the mistake of doing it to you again."

"That wasn't my point, but thanks." She sounded sad as she stood, and turned to walk away from him.

Peter jumped to his feet, caught her by the shoulders and spun her around. "What do you want from me?"

So much for a retreat.

"Just leave me alone, Peter. Stay out of my life, and I'll stay out of your life as well."

"That's not what I asked. Just tell me what you want."

She squirmed to break his hold on her shoulders. "What I want you can't give. It's not in your make-up."

"Maybe it's time to just do what I want then," he said more to himself than to her.

"Peter?"

His lips dropped to hers. She tasted . . . she tasted like stale coffee and those mints she was always popping. She tasted good in spite of, or maybe because of, it. She tasted right, and she felt even better, pressed against his body.

He wanted more, much more. But he was afraid more wouldn't be enough. The only thing that would be enough—

Suddenly it hit him what he was doing, and a nano-second later, Judy hit him on his left shoulder. It didn't hurt, but Peter got the point and reluctantly let go. "I'm sorry."

Judy rubbed her right fist in her left hand, eyeing him warily.

Peter thought he saw in her eyes something . . . no, it couldn't be. Judy didn't cry. Not his Judy.

Not that she was his or ever would be.

"I'm sorry," he said again, for lack of anything better to say.

"I'm sure you are." Her voice was a whisper.

"Jude."

"I'll see you tomorrow, Peter."

"That's it?"

She looked at him again, a look that tore at him. "Yes, that's it."

She left, and this time Peter didn't stop her. What

was going on? That damned contest and then the wedding, that's when things started getting strange. Well, it was over now, and things could get back to normal.

The kiss? That was a fluke. It was the grand finale in this weird little upheaval they'd been experiencing.

It didn't mean a thing. It wouldn't happen again.

No matter how much he'd like it to.

Peter O'Brien had kissed her.

And not just some little token peck on the cheek, but a out-and-out kiss.

Judy groaned as she sped her Lumina down the highway toward home. All she wanted to do was curl up in her house, and hide from the fact that Peter O'Brien had kissed her.

Worse, that she'd kissed him back.

Even worse, that she'd liked it.

Oh, how she had liked it.

Her body felt warm all over from just the thought. It wasn't right to like it.

He was her co-worker, nothing more.

Maybe he'd even file harassment charges against her. No, he'd kissed her first, so he was officially the first harasser, she was just the follow-up harasser.

And so what if she liked it?

She was going to forget that kiss, and forget all about the liking part. She wasn't going to dream about it, or think about it, or fantasize about what it might have been like to keep kissing him . . . to do more than kiss him.

No, she wasn't going to think about it.

Home.

She was going home, and she was going to blot this whole episode out of her mind, and do her utmost to blot it from her dreams as well. She was going to spend the rest of the day forgetting Peter O'Brien kissed her and that she'd liked it.

What she needed was distraction. She flipped on the radio and heard Cassie saying, "That was Cher, and this is Cassie Grant here. For those of you who aren't night owls, I'm WLVH's nighttime disc jockey. Yes, our manager pulled me out of a sound sleep to be here with all of you this afternoon. So, give me a call, and say hi. With your help, and a barrel of coffee, I just might make it through this shift. Here's an oldie, but goodie, for Lovehandle's own Punch and Judy."

The opening for "Close to You" started playing.

Cassie might look like a innocent pixie, but Judy decided that she was, in actuality, a demon sent to torment her.

Cassie had been spying out the window and seen them kiss. What was she hinting at with that song— that Judy wanted Peter? Nothing could be further from the truth. She might want to kill him from time to time, but she didn't *want* him.

And she didn't care about his kiss either.

No, not a bit. She would forget their one stupid kiss, no problem.

She was about to flip off the stereo when lights in her rearview mirror caught her eye. Flashing lights.

Darn.

She glanced at her speedometer and tried to remember what the speed limit was. She was pretty sure it was lower than what the needle read. She jabbed the brake, pulled to the side of the street, and unrolled the window.

Her life sucked.

The female officer walked to her window. "Ma'am, do you have any idea how fast you were going?"

"I didn't until I saw your lights, but I realize I was speeding." She flipped down her visor, and pulled her license from behind it.

She handed it to the officer. "Here."

The officer glanced at the license and then examined Judy with surprise in her eyes. "You're not going to offer any excuses?"

"I could try, but you and I both realize that nothing can justify breaking the law. I was speeding because I was distracted. That's no excuse. I could have hurt someone. I deserve the ticket."

The woman peered at the license. "You're Judy Bently? Judy from WLVH?"

She nodded. Just what her image needed, a police record.

"Listen, having someone admit they deserve what they get is a novelty. Let's just say this time is a warning, and you should be careful in the future."

"Officer—"

"Dana."

"Dana, I really deserve the ticket."

"And that you recognize the fact is enough for me. Let's not let it happen again, though, okay? You and Punch are my favorite way to start the day."

"So no ticket?" Judy felt almost disappointed.

Officer Dana must have seen it in her face because she asked with a laugh, "You really want one that bad?"

Judy sighed. "It would have been a perfect ending for a perfectly awful day."

"Maybe it's the turning point and things will get better from here?" The officer smiled a toothy, pleasant grin.

"Yeah, that's one possibility. Another possibility is that this is a momentary lull before the real trouble starts."

Dana laughed. "Honey—" She shook her head. "Good luck."

"Yeah, good luck she says." Judy drove away, this time well within the speed limit. "Luck would be Peter O'Brien taking a job somewhere, anywhere else."

But Judy was well aware that luck wasn't on her side.

Life stunk.

At least Judy's life stunk. Even more than the zoo in the middle of the afternoon on a sweltering August day. The summer humidity just made the smell so much worse.

She glared at Peter, sitting next to her in the cage. He didn't notice, of course; he was too busy talking to the crowd of women gathered around the cage. "Peter, we're on in five."

She put on her headset and watched the clock. "This is Judy Bently—"

Peter picked up right on cue. "—and Peter *Punch* O'Brien. We're here at the Erie Zoo on this bright August afternoon sitting in the alligator cage."

Judy forced a chuckle, knowing their listeners expected one. "Thankfully, the alligator is inside for the day. We're borrowing its cage, locked in it, as a matter of fact, to raise money for the zoo's renovation fund. Erie's blessed with its own zoo, and it's up to us to make sure it stays one of Erie's premiere attractions. With your help, we'll be able to make a difference for the animals and all the children who visit the zoo each year."

Peter picked up. "And with your help, we'll get out of this cage. Our promotion director, Ted Hyatt, has the key. He promised to let us out as soon as we've raised a thousand dollars—of course, we wouldn't mind making more." He laughed.

Peter probably had the sexiest laugh Judy had ever heard. The sound was one of the things that made him a great disc jockey.

Judy picked up the on-air banter. "Remember Al, from Big Al's Autos? He sponsored our 'Pickup Lines' contest, along with WLVH. A half hour ago, he just dropped off a check for two hundred dollars."

"Now, we don't expect everyone to match that amount, but remember, every little bit helps. As much as I love the zoo, I really don't want to spend the night in here." He paused a pregnant moment and added, "Though spending a night with Judy wouldn't be all that tough."

Judy smiled what she hoped was a convincing smile. It was so brittle she feared her face might crack.

In the studio it didn't matter if she smiled or not, but here, in front of a live audience, it did. "Fat chance of that ever happening, Punch, old boy. I'd rather take my chances with the alligator.

"In commemoration of our day at the zoo, here's an oldy, but goody. Hopefully, it will inspire you to come visit . . . and bring your checkbook."

Strains of "The Lion Sleeps Tonight" wafted over the WLVH speakers positioned around the cage.

Judy leaned over close to Peter, so none of their audience could hear and whispered, "Lay off the cracks about me and you, Peter, or I'll be parking my foot in your butt."

"Honey, get your mind off my butt and on your job." He smiled at the crowd. "So, anyone have any money to help us out here?"

A couple of Peter's female fans came forward and put small bills into the box.

Next in line was Barney Clark, Ethan's best man.

"Hi, Judy honey."

Judy smiled her first genuine smile of the morning. "Barney! You came to rescue me?" She hammed it up for the audience's benefit.

Barney played right along. He moved right in front of the cage and pressed his hand to his heart. "How on earth can I woo you if you're stuck in a cage with another man? I decided I need to get you out of the cage so I can ply you with my manly charms. So, I brought a check."

Judy accepted the check. When she looked at the check she laughed. "That's generous of you."

"Well, actually Ethan, of Westbrook Pharmacy is the generous one. He's still on his honeymoon, and so I made an executive decision. After all, WLVH helped him find his true love. I'm sure he'd want to help me find mine."

The crowd was eating up Barney's performance. Judy couldn't help but laugh along with them. Barney was too irrepressible. She doubted anyone could be annoyed with him. Unlike her unruly co-host, who was so very easy to become annoyed with. "Why don't you tell the audience how much the oh-so-generous Ethan Westbrook and Westbrook Pharmacy donated?"

"Three hundred dollars." The crowd clapped wildly. "With Big Al's and all the crowd's donations, you're only a hundred off, right?"

"Right." One hundred dollars and she'd be done with this absurd public display.

"Darlin'," Barney said, "here's my personal check for that hundred." He held it just out of reach. "On the condition you have dinner with me."

Judy didn't even pause a moment to think. She snapped up the check. "Dinner it is."

The crowd clapped wildly.

Peter leaned toward her and whispered in her ear. "Don't you think selling yourself is a bit extreme?"

"Selling myself?"

Ted Wyatt came forward with the key and unlocked the cage's door.

"Dinner with Barney for a hundred dollars. Seems to me there's a name for that."

Judy rose from her stool and faced Peter. "I'd have dinner with Barney, no strings attached, but if I can help out the community and have dinner, well, it's a plus."

"Fine, whatever." He glanced at their mobile panel. "We're on in twenty seconds."

"Then I'm out of here with Barney," she said.

Peter scowled.

She might not be romantically interested in Barney, but she knew she'd enjoy his company, and there was the added benefit that it annoyed Peter. An irritated Peter was easier to deal with than a kissing one.

Yes, she couldn't wait for dinner.

"This is Punch and Judy. We're here at the Erie Zoo, still sitting in the alligator cage." He gave a curt nod in Judy's direction.

She smiled at him as serenely as she could manage. "We may be sitting in the cage at the moment, but not for long. The cage is unlocked. You see, we just received a very generous check from Westbrook Pharmacy that put us within a hundred dollars of our goal. Barney Clark, a Westbrook employee, donated that hundred dollars from his personal checkbook, so we've met our goal."

Peter rolled his eyes. "He donated it on the condition our Judy go to dinner with him."

"I would have gone to dinner with Barney, donation or no donation. Sometimes a woman meets a man and she just know he's a keeper."

Looking at Punch she smiled. "And sometimes she meets one, and knows he just isn't."

Chapter Five

"You don't mind that I used you, do you?" Barney's smile was lopsided, the left side rose just a bit higher on his face than the right, and endearing.

They were sitting in an intimate corner of Waves, an exclusive Erie restaurant. Lanterns created an irresistible ambiance—small ones on the tables, larger ones on the wall—casting a pale, amber glow that washed the room. Seascapes, anchors, and fish tanks added the finishing touches. Rather than over-done, it gave the restaurant a romantic atmosphere.

Romance wasn't what was on Barney's or Judy's minds, though.

"Since we pretty much decided at Mary and Ethan's wedding that we weren't going to pursue a relationship, I figured there must be something up."

Judy smiled reassuringly. That he wanted to make sure he wasn't hurting her was sweet. "You certainly went about asking me out in a very big and public way. And I have a confession of my own."

"Oh?"

She grinned. "I used you too."

Rather than appear insulted, Barney leaned forward with interest shining in his eyes. "Want me to guess who?"

Judy shook her head. "I'm not really trying to make anyone jealous. I'm trying to convince someone I'm not interested."

She didn't know who she was trying to convince, Barney or herself. She didn't want to make Peter jealous. That would be an admission that she was interested, or that she thought he was.

No, neither one was really interested. That kiss was just a fluke—the fact she liked it an even bigger one. This date was an easy way to see that there was no more *fluking* between them.

"Does he have looks that would make a seraphim cry?"

"You're not going to let it go, are you?"

Barney's curls tumbled to and fro as he shook his head. He might not have a seraphim's good looks, but the curls lent him a cherubic sweetness.

Judy took a sip of her wine. "Peter." Saying his

name out loud seemed to make the kiss even more real.

"Peter O'Brien? As in Punch and Judy in the morning?"

She nodded miserably.

"And you don't want him, right?" The tone of Barney's voice said he didn't quite believe it.

Judy choked on her drink. "Not at all. I don't want to date him, don't want to kiss him, don't want to think about him anymore."

"You've dated him?"

"No." She shook her head for emphasis.

Barney's eyes narrowed. "You've kissed him?"

"Well . . ." She hesitated. "Well, not really."

"How not really?"

"He kissed me," she admitted.

"And you just stood there, all wooden, not responding at all?"

The feel of Peter's lips on hers played for the thousandth time in her mind. She hadn't wanted to respond. That should count for something. But she had responded, much to her dismay. "Maybe just a little."

"So, let me get this straight. You work with him, but you haven't dated him. And then there's the kiss you maybe a little responded to."

He steepled his fingers under his chin and rested his elbows on the table. "You've been thinking about him?"

Judy reached for her glass, lifted it, and rather than take a sip, set it back on the table. "I work with him, for pete's sake. Of course I think about him."

She didn't want to think about Peter, much less talk about him. Desperate to change the topic, she took a shot. "So who are you avoiding?"

The smile melted from Barney's face. "That doesn't matter."

"Come on. Turnabout's fair play." She slid her chair closer to his. "Who is she?"

"A woman."

"Well that's a relief. Does this woman have a name?" Turning the tables on him made her feel a little better.

Barney's scowl said he didn't feel better at all. "We've only gone out a couple times."

"But now you're out with me?" Judy wasn't sure she understood. Barney seemed more confused than she was, and that was saying something.

"I've never had anything move so fast. There was something different there. When I was with her . . . I don't know. It made me nervous."

"So you asked me out?" Just like a man. Sense something happening on more than a physical level and they all ran the other way.

He shook his head. "Well, not really. You see, she suggested we see other people."

"*She* suggested?" That didn't sound right. Barney was cute and sweet. A real catch. Unlike Peter,

Barney seemed to be a man who would stick around for more than a week.

"She suggested." Frustration tinged his voice. His back was ramrod straight in the chair. He glowered at her, as if Judy was somehow to blame for this woman's lack of sense.

Judy didn't take offense. She was too familiar with emotions that fluctuated wildly and unreasonably. At least since Mary and Ethan's wedding, she was becoming an expert. "But, you didn't want to get serious, so why are you upset?"

"I didn't want to get serious." He shrugged and added, "But I didn't want her seeing other guys."

"So, you asked me out, in a very public way, to teach her a lesson?"

"You think it will work?" There was an almost desperate plea in his voice.

Judy didn't think a woman who wanted to date other men would mind that Barney was dating other women, but she couldn't say so and dash his faint hopes. "Who knows? Tell you what, let's just forget about the people who make us crazy and enjoy the evening. No pressure, no confusion, just two friends enjoying a dinner together."

"I could use a simple evening. Things have been very complicated lately. So, tell me, how did the rest of the day go?"

Relief washed over Judy. An evening without discussing, or even thinking, about Peter O'Brien was just what the doctor ordered. "The rest of my day? It was a real *zoo*."

"That's bad." There was an almost desperate quality that echoed in their laughter.

"Everyone was *monkeying* around and it really got my *goat*."

"Honey, you really need a *keeper*." He squeezed her hand.

A sense of camaraderie filled Judy. Barney knew what she was going through, because he was there too.

That's how Peter found them, their hands touching, their faces lit with amusement. Trying to ignore them, he followed the maitre d' to his table. His arm tightened around Belinda's waist as he watched Judy hanging all over Barney.

Barney? What kind of name was that? Parents who would name their child Barney must have had a lot of latent hostility.

Peter was inclined to empathize with them, though there was nothing latent about his hostility. Barney annoyed the hell out of him.

He pulled out the chair with its back toward Judy's table, and held the chair out for Belinda. She glanced over her shoulder once before she took her seat.

Peter slid into his own perfectly positioned chair and saw Judy slide a little closer to Barney the Bozo.

"Did you see them?" he hissed at Belinda.

"So? She's a colleague, Peter. You haven't even

been on a date with her, unless it happened since I last talked to you."

"No date. I don't want to date her, but I don't want to see her hurt."

"You think Barney would hurt her?" Belinda peeked over her shoulder at the couple. She toyed with her water glass.

"You know the bozo?"

The ice in her water clinked against the glass as Belinda set it down with a thud. "We met at the wedding, remember?"

"So what do you think about him?" Peter contemplated Belinda's nervousness. There was something going on here.

"He . . ." she hesitated a moment. "He seems nice enough."

"I don't trust him."

"Why?" She toyed with her water glass again.

"Shifty eyes."

"Shifty eyes?"

Peter glanced at Judy's table again. "He's got a look about him that makes me suspicious."

"And that look resides in his shifty eyes?"

He leaned back and crossed his arms over his chest. "So, you've seen it too."

Belinda sighed. "Peter, you want Judy. So go after her. Lurking in the shadows, spying on her, isn't going to help."

"I'm not lurking, I'm having a meal with you."

"Yes, with me, a woman we decided you're not really interested in." She glanced over her shoulder again.

Peter didn't have to glance. He had a front row seat for the show. Barney and Judy were certainly having a good time. They were laughing again. What could be that funny, other than maybe Barney's ridiculous name?

"A woman you're not even listening to."

Peter pried his attention away from Judy. "I thought we were friends."

"We are friends. And I'm friend enough to tell you that this is getting weird." She jerked her head toward Judy's table. "Just ask her out."

"I doubt she'd go." It wasn't doubt, it was absolute certainty. She'd done everything except announce on the air that she wasn't interested. And, actually, she had even kind of done that too. "She got mad when I showed up at a game she was coaching."

"Game?"

"Girls' basketball, some summer program." The game brought to mind Bert with the great butt. Maybe Barney was preferable to Hank's wife setting Judy up. After all, Peter could see that Barney was goofy, which made him safer than the potentially great-butted Bert.

"She was mad you came to watch a basketball game?" Belinda eyes narrowed as she studied him.

Peter had a feeling Belinda wasn't going to let him

get away with evading anything tonight, so he answered honestly, "Actually, I think she was mad that I told all those basketball moms we were an item."

"I see."

Belinda managed to say a lot with those two little words. As a matter of fact, she said more than Peter wanted to hear. He shook his head, denying her silent accusation.

"No, you don't. I was saving her from a blind date. You know how hideous those are."

"Peter, we met on a blind date."

Women. They were always so literal. "That was different."

"And Mary and Ethan met on the ultimate blind date."

"That's just what *she* said." He couldn't tear his eyes from the table. She smiled at something Barney said.

"Judy was mad I might have made her miss the man of her dreams." Her anger that night wouldn't even begin to match what she'd do if Peter walked over to her table and demanded to know what she was smiling at.

"I see," Belinda said softly.

"And, maybe she was a little put out that I kissed her."

"Kissed her?" Belinda's full lips twitched as if she wanted to smile but was trying not to.

Peter glared. "I think the fact she kissed me back—big time kissed me back—is what really set her off though."

"And now we're tailing her date. Yes, I'm sure that's going to make a positive impression."

"I'm not tailing her. I'm having dinner with you." There Judy went, smiling at Barney again. This was getting out of hand. Peter tore his eyes from the tableau and faced Belinda. "Can I help it if we're eating at the same restaurant?"

Those blue eyes said Belinda wasn't buying it. Those eyes didn't even begin to register the annoyance Judy's lake blue ones would if she spotted him; of that, Peter was sure.

"And how did that happen? We just stumbled into the same place?"

He avoided Belinda's gaze. "Maybe I knew Barney asked her out, and maybe after about seventeen calls, I found out where he had reservations. After he asked her out in such a big way, I figured they were going somewhere nicer than fast food."

"You know, if your radio career falls through, you can always go into the private eye business."

"I don't think I'm doing so hot."

Judy leaned over and said something to Barney. As she looked up, her gaze met Peter's.

"Uh-oh," he muttered.

Judy walked across the floor to their table, Barney right behind her. "Peter. Imagine meeting you here."

"Yes. What a coincidence."

Belinda snorted.

Peter glared at his sort-of-date. She was supposed to be on his side, not making Judy stare at him with suspicion in her eyes.

"Well, we'll let you get back to your date," he said.

"What a surprise," Barney echoed.

He didn't look at Peter, but held Belinda in his line of sights. Sparks all but flew between them.

Peter felt sneaky suspicion begin to take shape. He watched the silent interplay between Barney and Belinda. "Now that we've discussed the vagaries of the universe, we'll let the two of you get back to your dinner," he announced.

Barney copped a grim semblance of a smile. "I have a better idea, why don't the four of us eat together?"

"Peter and I were hoping to be alone." Belinda's voice was full of significance.

"You can always be alone later." Barney sank into the seat next to her. "Come on Judy. Let's join them. The four of us will have a great time."

"Yeah, a great time," Peter muttered.

Barney flagged their server. "Could you bring our drinks over? We'll be finishing the meal with our friends here." Barney seemed to be the only one at ease. "So, what were we talking about?"

"Coincidences," Peter said.

Judy looked as if she could chew nails, as if chewing them would be preferable to sharing a meal with Peter.

"Yes, isn't it a coincidence that I'm out for dinner, and you just happened to pick the same place to eat?" Judy said as she accepted the inevitable and slid into her chair.

Barney scooted his chair closer to Judy, draping an arm over her shoulder. Peter's stomach tightened, and it was all he could do not to plow a fist into Barney's smug, goofy face.

Barney pulled Judy a little closer. "We've never been out with another couple, sweetheart. I think it's nice. You and Peter here work together all day but don't get a chance to really know each other social-ly. Look how nice you two got along at Mary and Ethan's wedding. I mean, watching you on the dance floor, you'd never know you guys worked together. I would have thought—"

Peter was afraid of where Barney was heading and supplied, "We're friends. At least I'd like to think we're friends, Jude."

The server handed Barney and Judy their drinks. "Yeah, friends," Judy said, in between sips.

Barney just ramrodded on with the conversation. "Belinda, how nice to see you again. I thought you told me at the wedding that you and Peter had decid-ed a relationship wasn't going to work?"

Peter slid his chair closer to Belinda's. It was as if there was an invisible line dividing the table into two warring camps. But, whenever there was a war, someone always wanted something the other person had, and he was very much afraid of what he wanted. He stared at Judy. *Who* he wanted. The want was growing by leaps and bounds with every passing second.

Belinda dropped a hand on Peter's knee. "When Peter called and invited me to dinner, I was surprised, but pleased. I know we'd decided to take a step back, but what woman can resist a man with Peter's looks and charm?"

Peter shot Belinda a look of gratitude. Too bad things between them hadn't worked out. She was a woman in a million.

"I can," Judy muttered.

"Can what?" Belinda asked.

"Resist him." She paused a moment, then added for emphasis, "Boy, can I."

Peter shot her an angry glare. "You're certainly working hard enough to prove it. The question is, just who are you trying to convince, me or yourself?"

"What do you mean by that?" Judy challenged.

It was if Barney and Belinda ceased to exist. The only person Peter was aware of was Judy. "I mean, you sell yourself to a man you don't care about for a hundred dollars, just to prove you don't want me, when your kiss proved just the opposite."

"My kiss? You mean that disgusting display? If I wanted a kiss, I'd kiss Barney. At least he has the decency to take me out before he makes his moves."

"Moves? You think that pathetic kiss we shared constitutes my moves? Honey, just ask Belinda about my moves. That was nothing."

Belinda started to reply, but Judy cut her off. "I'll say it was nothing. Nothing I want to experience again. From now on, you just keep your lips, your tongue, and your dates to yourself. I don't want anything to do with any of them."

Peter slid his chair closer to Judy. "That's what you say, but when you kissed me back, it said something different."

"Kissed you back?"

"Yeah, when you did that little moany thing in the back of your throat."

"That moan? That was me gagging."

"Gagging?" He had kissed a number of women in his life and none had ever gagged—Judy included.

"Yes, gagging. You're a womanizer, Peter, and I'm worth more than you're able to give."

"It would be a night you'd never forget."

"I'm sure I wouldn't." She braced her hands against the table. "I'd be having nightmares for years to come." She fired the shot with a marksman's accuracy.

"Nightmares? Honey, a night with me is a night women all over the world fantasize about." He suddenly remembered his date. "Tell her, Belinda."

Belinda shook her head and slid her chair toward Barney. "I must confess, I've never spent a night with him, and I didn't find myself spending much time dreaming about one. I guess things just never clicked that way for us. We're better friends than we would have been lovers."

Peter glared at Belinda.

The woman was a traitor. She knew why they were out and yet she didn't play her role very well. Actually she didn't play it at all.

"Thanks, Belinda. I was willing to let Barney think you couldn't live without me and not tell him you're out with me because you're afraid of what's going on between the two of you." It was a stab in the dark, but the look in Belinda's eyes said it was accurate.

Barney closed the space between them. "You did this to make me jealous?"

He captured Belinda's chin in his hand, and turned her face to his.

Belinda nodded miserably. "I don't understand what's going on between us. I've never felt like this before."

"Sometimes you just know something's right. You can fight against it and waste precious time, or—"

"Or?" Belinda whispered.

"Or you can take it as a gift and celebrate it."

Belinda nodded and whispered, "Maybe I was wrong about dating other people."

"No doubt about it, lady. You belong with me." He stood, took her hand, and helped Belinda to her feet.

Barney suddenly seemed to remember Judy. "You don't mind?"

Judy smiled. "Go ahead, I'm happy for you and Belinda."

Peter watched Barney lean over, give Judy a fraternal kiss, and then wrap his arm around Belinda and lead her from the restaurant.

Judy watched them as well. When they were out of sight, she stood. "Well, that's that. Goodnight, Peter."

"Sit down."

She shook her head. "I don't think so."

He grabbed her hand and physically pulled her into her seat. "Oh, but I do."

"Peter, the only thing between us is a working relationship."

"We have a working relationship only because you're too afraid to take it further. You know you'd like to take it further."

All his doubts about whatever was between them faded, at least for the moment. He hadn't released her hand. It felt frail in his. It felt right.

Judy yanked her hand from his grasp, as if she'd read his mind and didn't approve. "You and your giant, over-inflated ego would like to think so, wouldn't you?"

She started rifling through her purse.

"You can't disguise the way you reacted to me."

Maybe that was what was attracting him. Her mixture of desire and alarm were intoxicating.

"You're right. I might not be able to disguise it, I can control it. I'll be the first to admit you make a pretty package." She tossed a twenty on the table and rose. "But a woman—a real woman—wants more than a bauble. She wants a man of substance, someone who's more than one-dimensional."

Peter reached for her hand. "Honey, I guarantee substance."

Judy pulled away. "Peter, like I said, a real woman wants more than a bauble, and I don't think you have more in you." She started toward the door.

Peter took out a wallet, tossed a few more bills on the table, and followed her outside the restaurant. "You don't know me, don't know a thing about me." He swung her around, so she was facing him. "How can you judge who I really am?"

She squirmed, trying to break free of his arms, but Peter held firm.

"You're a womanizer, a man who is used to being admired for the shell he wears, not what's inside." There was a sadness in her voice.

"You don't have that problem?" He'd seen how men panted around her. Barney was a prime example.

Anger flared in those blue eyes. "Don't try your absurd brand of . . . what would you call it? Flattery?"

"What do you want from me? What do you want from me?"

Judy shook her head. "That's the second time you've asked me that question, Peter."

"And it's the second time you haven't given me an answer."

"All I want is for things to be the way they were before the wedding. Whatever is going on, this pursuit you feel obligated to—"

"Obligated? Why would I feel obligated to pursue you?"

"How would I know?" She couldn't understand her recent confusion over Peter, so how could she be expected to understand his pursuit? "Maybe it's because I'm the first woman who's actually been immune to your charm?"

"Immune?" He reached out and brushed her hand with his own. "That's what you call it?"

Judy rubbed her hand against her dress, trying to erase the reaction that shook her at his merest touch.

"Immune," she lied.

She saw his intent in his eyes but couldn't seem to draw away. He drew her into his arms, cornering her between the wall and his body.

"Peter, I think this would be a mistake."

"Honey, if you're as immune as you say," his lips brushed against the base of her neck, "this should be a piece of cake."

"I don't want a piece of anything you have, thank you very much." Her voice sounded breathless.

"Give me a minute." This time his lips traced her collarbone. "And then tell me what you want."

Chapter Six

Judy sought Peter's eyes, needing to know what he was feeling, needing to convince herself that this was . . .

She couldn't fill in a word. That was the problem. She didn't know what she wanted to believe *this* was.

"Peter?" she whispered.

He answered her unasked question by kissing her.

Judy knew she should remain immune like she'd claimed to be. Problem was, she was a liar. A huge liar.

She wasn't immune to Peter. She'd been attracted to him when they first started working together. She'd done her best to forget it, but she couldn't. He did something to her, something she didn't quite understand and didn't really want to learn to understand. Some things were just better left alone.

Only the taste of him was impossible to ignore.

She wanted more.

Letting go of her restraints, Judy allowed herself to lose herself in the marvel of Peter's lips on hers. She finally allowed herself to return the kiss.

He tasted like everything she ever wanted.

But some people were only allowed a glimpse of heaven before the pearly gates slammed shut. She withdrew her lips from Peter, and pushed against his chest. "Peter, this was a mistake."

"Honey, the only mistake has been all the time you—" Judy bristled and Peter obviously saw it because he hastily changed his wording. "—we've wasted. I want you, you want me. Oh, you can deny it all you want, but your body says different. We're free and unattached adults and there's no reason we can't pursue these feelings."

"Except the fact we work together," she said softly. He still held her. She knew she should break the contact, that it would be safer, but she couldn't seem to move from the shelter of his arms.

"Listen, I've been warning myself away from you for the same reason. But we're both adults. We could make this work. There's no reason an off-air relationship should mess up work." His arms tightened.

"And when the relationship is over?" she whispered into his shirt.

Peter fingers brushed her chin, pulling her to face him. "Belinda and I dated, but now we don't. We're still friends. You and I could still be friends as well."

"I don't know if you can call what we've had a friendship."

"I think you're wrong. We butt heads, and you tend to spend a lot of time calling me on the carpet, but under all that, I consider myself your friend, Judy. You see me as I am and won't let me get away with anything. I like that. There's no reason when we decide it's over that we can't still work together."

"Peter, I know there's some fundamental flaw with your reasoning, but darned if I can think of it."

So many emotions. Judy couldn't sort them out and make sense out of them.

"You exasperate me more than any other living person, but—"

"Leave it right there, Jude. That way I can imagine the long list of compliments you were going to give me."

"You don't have to imagine. You're smart, quick-witted, and funny. But you build walls and don't let anyone get too close. I'm afraid if we dated, I'd hit my head on the wall and get hurt," she admitted softly. "I'm not that tough."

"Listen, Jude, no matter how it looks, I don't want to rush you. Maybe I do put up barriers, but you're already closer to me than any woman I know. The fact we're seeing each other in a different light means something. Let's take time to find out what. Let's just not say no to the possibilities I think we're both seeing. We can date, spend some time together."

Despite her misgivings, the idea was tempting. Maybe if she spent some non-work time with Peter she could get over her infatuation.

"Dating, huh? Like you come to my house with chocolates and flowers, then we go to dinner and a show?"

"I've never done chocolates and flowers, but dinner and a show, well, that could be arranged."

"And if after we've dated, if I say, really, I'm not interested, you'll back off and we'll go back to just working together?"

All the humor went out of his face as he nodded. "If, after we've dated, that's how you feel, we'll just shake hands and go back to being 'Punch and Judy in the morning.' "

She extended a hand. "Deal."

Rather than shaking it, Peter drew it to his lips and kissed her palm. "Deal."

"This wasn't part of the deal," Judy protested a few days later.

She glanced down at the plain black tank bathing suit, thankful she was safe within the confines of the van until it was time to start the day's embarrassment.

"You said no suit at the beach, not at the gelatin slide." Ted perused her body and grinned. "And, I think the audience will more than appreciate the outfit."

"I can't go out in public like this." She tugged at the bottom of the suit. As soon as her hand was removed, it slid back up.

"Well, you can't do it in street clothes."

She reached in her bag, took out her cut-off jean shorts and shimmied them over the bathing suit. Next she pulled out a WLVH t-shirt. "There."

Ted's brow furrowed. "You'll ruin them."

"I've got tons of holey jeans I can cut off any time I need a new set of shorts."

"The t-shirt then."

She flashed him a wry smile. "I know the boss. I bet I can get another one."

"Fine. Do whatever you want. You always do." Ted clambered out of the WLVH van.

"Okay, I will," she called after him, waving just to annoy him even more. Ted annoyed her often enough.

She smiled as she watched him stomp off toward the pool of slimy red gelatin. That was the problem with swimming in gelatin—it never got cold enough for the stuff to solidify. It was a real mess.

But not even a pool of gelatinous ooze could dim her spirits. She knew if she looked in a mirror the reflection would show her goofy grin. But she didn't even try to hide it.

Peter O'Brien.

Who would have thought?

Well, Cassie claimed to have thought, and even Barney and Belinda, who were practically in each other's pockets, claimed to have thought Peter and Judy had possibilities.

But Judy had never thought.

Maybe she'd dreamed about Peter occasionally, but she hadn't carried those dreams into daylight hours. If she'd let herself dwell on them, she would never have been able to function.

Now they were dating. The idea took some getting used to. After their gelatin dive they were going out to dinner. Part of Judy was excited at the thought, part was scared spitless.

Her mass of conflicting emotions hadn't straightened itself out since dinner with Barney and Belinda. But despite doubting the wisdom of dating Punch, despite the fear she was going to end up with a broken heart, despite it all, she just couldn't help the goofy grin.

A knock on the van's door pulled her back to reality. She slipped on her sandals and opened the door.

"Peter." She felt all of sixteen every time she saw him. Her mouth went dry, her palms started to sweat and her ability to form a coherent sentence evaporated. "Did you want something?"

She almost groaned. Of course he wanted something. What a stupid thing to say. He wouldn't be knocking on the van's door if he didn't want something.

"I thought maybe you were going to hide in the van all day, and I came to see if there was a problem." He held out a hand.

Judy took it and jumped lightly to the ground. "I just finished changing."

"I heard. Ted's annoyed you won't wear the suit." His grin said he enjoyed annoying Ted as much as she did. He took her hand and led her toward the gelatin.

They'd set their gelatin on the bayfront in the Pepsi Amphitheater. The perfect place for a summertime open air concert or community gathering. But it wasn't the perfect location to swim in gelatin.

No place was.

"I'm wearing the bathing suit, just under the shorts and shirt. There was no way I was wearing just the suit in public. He had the WLVH logo on it, but the logo almost covered the entire thing. The legs are cut clear to my belly button. And the top? Well, if I had any cleavage it would be showing."

"If you want, you could show it to me. I'll offer a tie-breaking opinion." His eyes moved up and down her clothes, as if he was Superman with x-ray vision. He winked.

Judy felt a surge of warmth spread through her body. She shook her head to clear it. She wouldn't be, couldn't be just another conquest for her Casanova partner. "I don't think that would be wise."

"Maybe it's time you stop thinking." He rested his arm over her shoulder and pulled her tight.

"Actually, I think now is the time that I need to concentrate on what my head is saying, not what my hormones are saying."

"Party pooper."

She grinned. "You said you knew me, but since you missed this fact, I'll confess my secret right up front—Party Pooper is my middle name."

"Come on. The crowd is gathering."

"I can't wait." She followed him into the crowd.

"It could be fun," he called over his shoulder.

Judy caught up with him. "I'm already going out with you, so you don't have to try and impress me by pretending to be Pollyanna Peter. I miss my sarcastic, acerbic Punch."

He wiped his brow in mock relief. "Good. This being a nice, upbeat guy was killing me." He walked up the three steps to the platform.

She followed reluctantly, eying the red muck. "I don't think I want to do this."

Actually, she was sure she didn't want to do it.

"Too late." Peter led her to the microphone where Ted paced nervously.

"Where have you been?" His eyes took in Judy's change of clothes and he scowled.

"Working up the nerve to do this ridiculous show." Judy shot Ted one of her best glares and then turned to the crowd and smiled as she picked up her mike.

"Welcome everyone to the first annual 'WLVH Slide with Erie Pride.' Today, we're raising money for Erie's new outdoor ice skating rink. The city has donated the land, now it's up to the community to do their share. Here's Mayor Bowers to tell us a little more."

An average looking man whose most distinguishing feature was the grey business suit he wore to almost every occasion—even a gelatin swim, obviously, took the microphone from Judy. "Erie has a lot to be proud of . . ."

As the mayor spoke she moved toward the back of the stage, next to Peter. She leaned close and whispered, "I'm glad he's taking the first plunge."

"You prefer *used* gelatin?" he whispered back.

"I prefer no gelatin."

His shoulder brushed hers. Such a little thing shouldn't send her heart rate rocketing, but it did. She moved a fraction of an inch to his side, trying to put some distance between them.

"Gelatin makes you grumpy. You know that?"

"Do you want to break our date for tonight?" she asked, hope in her voice.

Peter chuckled. "No, I kind of think you're sexy when you're pouting."

"Grumpy, not pouting."

"Either way, you're cute."

"Shhh," Ted hissed.

Peter leaned even closer. She could smell his

cologne. He smelled good, he looked good. Everything about Peter was good, except the way he made her feel. It annoyed her how easily he could affect her. "To be cute you have to be under five-foot-five. I stopped being cute in fifth grade."

"Honey, I can't imagine you not being cute."

"Shhh," Ted admonished them again.

The mayor was winding down and Judy stepped back up to the microphone. "Thank you Mayor Bowers. Are you ready to take the first dive?"

"As ready as I'll ever be."

"Do you need to go change?" She eyed the grey suit that she was sure didn't come off any rack.

"I'm ready as is." He reached into his jacket pocket. "As the mayor, I saw to it the city donated the land. But as a citizen of Erie, I want to do my part too. Here's my personal check." He handed it over to Judy.

The mayor gamely walked to the slide.

"Let's give the mayor our support." She began clapping a rhythmic beat as he climbed the ladder. At the top, the mayor paused, bowed to the audience, and sat down. The clapping grew louder as he slid down the slide. He landed with a squish that more than convinced Judy she wasn't looking forward to her turn.

"Way to go Mayor Bowers! Now, who's next?" A line formed. One by one, they handed Peter checks and cash, then took their turn.

"Barney?" she asked with delight as her pretend date made his way to the front of the line.

"Clark," Peter said with a brisk nod.

Barney didn't seem to notice Peter's lack of enthusiasm as he smiled at Judy. "Ethan's not back until tomorrow, so I decided that he should make one more good donation before I'm done as manager."

"What does his father say?"

"He's so caught up in Gilda that he just smiles and nods at everything I ask."

Judy chuckled. "We'll gladly take Ethan's money. Have a ball."

Punch and Judy were scheduled to be last and she held out hope that maybe the crowd would all leave before she was forced to take the plunge. It was unrealistic, but Judy willingly clutched at straws.

Barney moved off and climbed the ladder. Judy spotted Belinda in the crowd and waved. All too soon there was no one left in line, but the crowd still remained.

"Well, Punch, looks like it's our turn," Judy said into the microphone.

"And I can tell you're looking forward to it."

"I'll confess I prefer warm water to lukewarm gelatin."

She stepped down the stage and climbed the ladder, Peter right behind her.

"Wait your turn," she said.

"I rather enjoy the view."

She looked down at him. "You're impossible."

"You knew that, but you're going out with me anyway." When he smiled it was hard to remember what she was annoyed about. It was hard to remember anything at all.

Judy stood at the top of the ladder. "Maybe I'll get a headache."

"Rumor has it that women save that for after the date, and before the big plunge."

"Plunge this!" She pushed off hard, not giving herself time to change her mind. Judy whizzed down the ten foot slide screaming, hit the gelatin with a *plunk* and then sunk. She rose, her mouth full of slime, her body coated in it.

The crowd cheered. Judy looked up just in time to see Peter barreling down the slide like a runaway cannonball. A cannonball heading directly at Judy.

"Peter!" she screamed just before he hit her and carried her back under the slime.

Her mouth once again filled and this time, her eyes were wide open and stinging.

She rose just in time for Peter to wrap his arms around her, pinning her arms at her side. She wasn't sure if it was a romantic ploy, or self-preservation, but she slugged him just to be on the safe side. "You rat."

He tsked his tongue at her and whispered, "We have an audience, darling."

Judy squirmed to get out of his grasp.

"Let me help you out," he said loud enough for the crowd to hear and appreciate his gallantry.

Judy allowed herself to be led to the edge of the pool and then she reached out a foot and tripped him. As Peter slid under the gelatin, she scrambled out of the pool. The crowd went wild.

Peter sputtered red gelatin. "That was nasty."

"That was for pushing me down the slide."

She took the towel that Ted handed her, and eyed her very clean and dry tormentor. She squished back to the mike as Peter crawled out. "I want to thank everyone for coming today. But, before we all go, I'd like to have the audience show their appreciation for WLVH's own promotions director, Ted Hyatt. Ted?"

Ted waved a hand as the audience dutifully clapped.

"Ted, you've done so much for all of us today. I think it's just a shame you didn't get a chance to try the slide."

"Maybe next year," he called with a tight laugh.

Judy sensed his nervousness and went for the kill. "Ted, why should you have to wait until next year? The pool's here, and the audience would love to see you take the plunge."

"I didn't get any sponsors."

Judy grinned triumphantly and reached a hand into her cut-off's pocket and pulled out a hundred dollar bill—a rather reddish looking bill, but still negotiable currency. "Ted, I'd be delighted to sponsor you."

The audience went wild clapping. Ted's dough-boy complexion took on a reddish hue that had nothing to do with the gelatin. He waved to the audience and kicked off his sneakers, then bowed to the inevitable.

As Ted climbed the slide, Judy caught Peter's eye and the look that shot between them was a private one, one that made Judy momentarily forget the red ooze that was drying on her body. One that made her forget the couple hundred onlookers. One that made her feel beautiful and desirable despite her current condition.

It was a look that spoke of trouble.

"Ted will never forgive you," Peter said for the hundredth time. He enjoyed taunting Judy, watching her blue eyes flash with annoyance, or warm with humor.

They were sitting at Waves again, this time on the outdoor deck that overlooked Erie's bay. This time without Belinda or Barney.

Peter couldn't believe he missed them, but he did. With their two cover-up dates there would have been some shielding, but now they were on their own, and he didn't have the slightest clue what to do.

This time his teasing invoked humor.

"I like to live on the wild side," she said.

Thinking of Judy's wild side made Peter's mouth go dry. He took a sip of beer to lubricate his arid throat. "When Ted starts planning our next public engagements, you just remember those words."

It was as if the wheels of conversation had come to a grinding halt. Peter studied Judy as she stared out at the bay. What were they doing?

He'd dated many beautiful women, and though Judy didn't feel she fit in the category, Peter did. But despite his experience, he didn't have a clue what to do with her. No matter how he tried, he couldn't pin her down. She was funny and brash on-air, but now that he was looking closer, he'd found a vulnerable, unsure side.

Beautiful and unsure.

She was sexy, but not in a sequined gown sort of way. No, he'd never seen anyone as sexy as Jude coaching her basketball team, or sliding into red gelatin.

Peter knew he was playing with fire.

For years he'd avoided dating women who wanted a commitment. He'd been committed enough to ask a woman to marry him, but that was long ago, and he'd learned his lesson.

He'd been fresh out of college, working as a DJ for a small upstate New York station. She'd been the station director, five years his senior. He'd thought what they had was something special. When he'd proposed, *special* wasn't how she seemed to feel. She treated his offering of his heart and marriage like a big joke. She'd laughed.

Oh, Peter had laughed too, but it hadn't been a joke, unless the joke was on him. Working with Shelia, day after day, had been terrible. She'd never seen beyond his face and for a while, he'd thought his looks were a curse.

Eventually, he'd learned to never get too close, to never be vulnerable.

Until now.

He should stop whatever was happening between him and Judy now, while he could. He should put things back on a professional level. That would be the smart thing to do.

He looked at Judy, the lake played her backdrop, the setting sun framed her in a golden glow. As he studied her, he realized that the fire he was playing with had already burned him. He wasn't sure if he could find a way to tear himself away from her heat. And he didn't think he wanted to try.

He wanted her in a way that he'd never wanted anything or anyone. Not even Marybeth Larson, the first girl he'd ever really fallen for.

Those on-air sparks they'd been giving off for the last year were just a sign of what actually blazed inside him. Something deeper and hotter.

"Are you as uncomfortable as I am?" Judy asked, breaking the silence.

"More so," he answered honestly.

"So what do we do?" She was still looking at the bay, avoiding his gaze.

Peter reached over, cupped her chin in his hand and gently forced her gaze to meet his. "What do you want to do?"

"That's the problem. What I want to do, and what I know I should do, are at odds."

"So, do we call it quits now, or do we take a chance and finish the date?"

Part of him, the part that had avoided becoming too involved with any woman, especially one he worked with, especially someone like Judy, wanted her to tell him to take her home. But one look in those grey-blue eyes, and he knew the date wasn't over, because neither of them was in the mood to be smart.

"Whoever said disc jockeys were wise. Let's go for it," she said quietly.

Peter waved down the waiter. "Let's order and then we'll go for a walk along the bay."

"You're on."

They talked and laughed, as if the ice were suddenly broken. A part of Judy's mind kept whispering that more than ice risked being broken, but she pushed the thought aside and let herself enjoy the moment.

"Hey, that's mine," she cried with a laugh as Peter speared her linguine.

"Guess I owe you a bite." Deftly he slipped the stolen linguine into his mouth. His lids lowered as he savored the flavor, chewing slowly, swallowing, and then washing the bit down with a long sip of wine.

Judy watched in fascination. She wished he was stealing tastes of her, not just her linguine. He'd start at her neck and nibble his way down, slowly, savoring each bite. And she'd let him. Boy, how she'd let him. And when he was done, she'd insist turnabout was fair play and she'd begin to sample . . .

"Here." Peter had cut a bit of prime rib and speared it. He leaned toward her and held the fork to her lips.

Judy's skin tingled, running hot, then cold. She took the bite, though the prime rib could have been cardboard for all she tasted it. It was just a bite of food, she reprimanded herself.

If a simple bite of steak, and lurid fantasies about what she'd like to be biting could make her body shiver with desire, what would it be like if he—

"Good?" he asked, interrupting her internal revery.

"Mmm," was the most coherent response she could manage. Images of Peter and what he would do with her, if she'd let him, if she asked him, if—

"Want more?"

She shook her head and tried to concentrate on her linguine. Linguine was much safer than Peter O'Brien.

"So, what should we talk about? Work?" Her voice sounded odd to her own ears.

Peter shook his head. "We're on a date, not at a business meeting. Why don't you tell me about how you ended up coaching basketball? Are you going to continue during the school year too?"

She talked about herself on the show, but never like this, at least not with Peter. She wasn't quite sure how to manage a real conversation. But basketball was a subject she knew inside and out.

"I played in grade school and high school. Coaching just seemed the next step." It came out in a rush, but she'd managed one coherent sentence. Maybe she could manage more?

"You didn't play college ball?"

She fidgeted with her linguine, twirling it on her fork, but not actually taking the bite.

"I was a decent high school player, but I didn't quite have what it took to play college ball. Maybe if I'd gone to a smaller school, I could have." Time to put the shoe on the other foot. "Did you play sports in school?"

"Soccer. It was the geek sport back then. Soccer players didn't get the same response from the girls as football and basketball players did."

Judy wasn't buying it. "With your looks? You weren't lacking for dates."

She pushed her plate back, suddenly unable to eat another bite.

"I'm sure you had the same problem."

For just a moment she flashed back to that tall, gangly girl who no boy ever looked at.

Shy, reserved, towering over her peers—Peter was right—Beanpole Bently never had to worry about dates. She'd never had any. She'd worked hard to overcome her shyness and grow past her youth, but she wasn't always sure she'd succeeded.

"Too many dates is definitely one problem I didn't have in school. Boys didn't notice me like that. They went for the pretty girls, the cute girls. I wasn't either."

"You're doing it again." He reached for her hand.

Judy pulled back, needing to keep her physical distance from Peter. "Doing what? Telling the truth?"

"Downplaying your looks."

"I'm sure many of your dates want to have flowery prose tossed at their feet, but I don't need them. I know what I am, and I'm comfortable with it."

Yes, Beanpole Bently knew exactly who and what she was. With his blinding good looks, Peter couldn't understand. Every woman over the age of ten stared at him when he entered a room. He couldn't have a clue how the other half—her half—lived.

He pushed back his plate. "Are you done?"

Judy wasn't sure if he was talking about the conversation or the meal, but either way, she was more than done and nodded.

Peter tossed some bills on the table, stood and pulled out her chair.

"Come on." He took her elbow and led her down the deck's stairs.

"Where are we going?" Judy usually had no problem keeping pace with anyone, but she had to hustle to keep up with Peter as he practically dragged her to the parking lot.

"We're going somewhere we can settle this once and for all."

"Settle what, how?" Judy didn't know what to make of the look on his face.

"Settle it," he said flatly. They reached his car in record time. "Get in."

Judy looked at him and wasn't sure who the man was she was seeing. The Peter she had worked with for the last twelve months was impersonal.

The Peter she'd been dealing with since Ethan and Mary's wedding was confusing mass of mixed signals. There was nothing mixed about Peter now. He was a man who knew what he wanted. This man was a stranger. She wasn't sure if the adrenaline racing through her system was fear, or something else she didn't want to name.

"Get in," he repeated.

Judy slid into the seat. She reached for her seatbelt and barely had it in place when the car roared to life. "Where are we going?"

He glanced her way and threw the car into reverse. "Trust me."

Chapter Seven

T rust him?

Peter was light years beyond her experiences. Judy didn't have the faintest idea how to deal with him, much less how to trust him. She'd watched his relationships with other women long enough to know trusting Peter was even more foolish than allowing him to come too close.

Trust him?

Despite what Peter said, Judy understood the basic truths about herself. She was bright, though not brilliant. She was passably good looking most days. But she'd never be anything more than middle-of-the-road. She'd been a decent basketball player, but nothing more. All in all, she was average, nothing exciting.

The car slowed down in front of a large brick apartment building. Judy eyed it nervously. "Where are we?"

"My place." He got out of the car and walked around to her door, opening it for her. He offered her his hand.

Judy took it reluctantly. Touching Peter was dangerous. "Isn't this college housing?" She dropped his hand as if it burned.

"Across, the street is." He jerked his head toward identical brick buildings opposite his. "This isn't the college's, though most of the tenants are students. I didn't even know about the college when I moved in."

"You didn't realize you were moving into a predominantly college area?" She remembered what college dorms were like. She was torn between humor and pity. The humor of the situation won out and she laughed.

"Not a clue. Remember I started last July? I thought I'd lucked into a quiet little apartment complex."

Peter's arm was around her shoulder. Judy didn't remember just when he'd put it there as he maneuvered her toward the door. "When did you realize your mistake?"

"August. Kids started moving in by the droves. It wouldn't be so bad, but we're across the street from college property. None of their rules apply."

"Let me guess." Images of her college days

flashed through her memory. "A one-word summary might be, party?"

"You've got it." He smiled then.

Darn, Judy wished he wouldn't do that. It did odd things to her knees. She'd heard the expression "weak in the knees," but had never experienced the phenomenon until the first time he had smiled at her, just over a year ago. She'd done her best to overcome the problem and had managed quite nicely, until lately.

"A party. Is that where you're taking me? A neighbor's party?" He could take her anywhere but to his place. She couldn't fight her growing need any longer and was afraid if he took her someplace where they were alone, she'd rip his clothes off and have her way with him.

And, oh, what a way it would be.

Peter was watching her intently. "No, not a party. It's time to get things straightened out between us. I want someplace more private than the restaurant or work."

They entered the building and Peter steered her to the stairway to the right.

Private? She had to control herself. There would be no one else to do it. She searched for something else to talk about besides her growing need to see him naked. "Second floor walk up?"

"Third. The good part about it is that it puts me above most of the noise." He took her arm, as if sensing her growing apprehension.

Judy stopped cold. "Peter, I don't think—"

"Don't think. We're just going to talk."

"I don't know if that would be wise. Actually, I think this whole date thing was a mistake. I should go home." She turned as if to start back down the stairs. Peter held tight.

"Talk. We don't have to do anything you don't want to do." His voice was cajoling, caressing. He tugged at her arm. "We need to settle this, Jude."

How was she supposed to go about telling Peter how she felt when she wasn't sure herself? She wanted him, but Peter was attractive enough that she was pretty sure that he was used to that.

That she had a slight crush on him? Well, that was pretty much old news as well. He led her down a hall, not loosening his grip.

"Afraid I'll run away, Peter?"

"Honey, I'm not letting go of you until we get this settled."

"I have no idea what you're talking about."

"But you will." He stopped in front of apartment 308. "Here we are, home sweet home." He reached in his pocket, pulled out his keys and opened the door. "Come in."

"Said the spider to the fly." He shut the door and Judy jumped at the loud thud that echoed the beat of her frantic heart rate. "So now what?"

He took a step toward her. "So, now we talk." He reached for her.

"Peter, unless I'm mistaken, talking's not what you have in mind."

"Well, there's talk, and then there's *talk*." He pulled her into his arms. "I don't want you to go."

Her voice dropped. "I don't really want to go."

"We have to give this a try. Maybe we can get it out of our systems." His lips came toward hers.

Judy knew she should say no and walk away without a backward glance. Kissing Peter was dangerous and foolish. But instead she found herself saying, "Yes."

"Are you sure?" he asked.

In any other circumstances, Judy would have laughed at the absurdity of the question, but as it was, she could find no humor in the circumstance. "No, I'm not sure. I still think that if touching you is a mistake, then kissing you is an even bigger one, but . . ." her voice trailed off.

"*But*. That's where I keep ending up as well. All the reasons—valid reasons—I have for keeping our relationship strictly professional all go to hell in a handbasket when I hit that *but*."

"So, what do we do if this doesn't work out?"

"We're both adults, we behave like adults. Right now, I don't want to think about what happens when this is over, not when we haven't even begun. And, speaking of beginning . . ."

His lips descended, and for once Judy was thankful for her height, because she was able to minimize the distance he had to travel. She met him halfway. The connection was nothing short of electric. Nothing had ever prepared her for the jolts of desire that exploded within her, nothing could have. It was like being given oxygen after being submerged in water for too long. Submerged for a lifetime.

Judy's hands wrapped around his neck attempting to get closer, needing to be closer. "Peter."

All her needs, all her longings wrapped up in that one word, in this one man.

He pushed and held her by her shoulders at arms length. "I don't understand this."

Feelings of need warred with nerves. She didn't understand this change in their relationship any more than Peter did. But she knew she could not let this—whatever *this* was—go any further than kissing.

"I . . ." She wasn't sure what to say.

A loud knock on the door saved her from searching for the words. "Someone's at your door," she said, stating the obvious with a sense of relief.

"And they can stay there. This is a two-person party. No party crashers." He tugged at her hand and another round of thudding came from the door.

"Maybe it's important."

Peter's face tightened into a scowl. "There's nothing that important. I can't think of a single person I need to talk to."

"You'd better get it." She was honest enough with

herself to realize that she wanted—no, needed—the reprieve.

She needed a moment to sort things out. Judy wasn't the type to jump into things. She was a thinker, a plodder. Average. "Really, you'd better get it."

Recognizing that whoever was at the door wasn't leaving and Judy wasn't going to let go, Peter marched to the front door with all the enthusiasm of a man marching to a firing squad.

"What?" he barked as he threw the door open.

"Party," came a chorus of three's response. Three very brawny looking men—maybe boys, she mused—stood in the hallway, beer steins in hand. "Come on, Pete. We're all back, and we've got a big poker game in the works."

Peter groaned. "It can't be time for school to start."

"You missed us. You know you did."

"Sure, as much as I missed that bunion the doctor took off last year. Now, go away."

The tallest of the group pushed forward. "Hey, looks like the O'Brien's got a new babe."

"What happened to the redhead?" the shortest, a bald mack truck of a young man asked.

The middle-sized one, a skinny man, laughed. "She was old news before the term ended. Keep up, Stallone."

The tall one walked over to Judy. "Honey, when O'Brien's done with you, look me up and I'll show you how a real man operates." He extended his non-beer-mugged hand. "Jonathan Keeper, a real Keeper, the ladies all assure me."

"Ah, Keep, he's all talk, no show. One of those basketball nerds. Me, I'm football, a manly sort of sport. They call me Stallone."

"Because it's your name, or is it a nickname?" Judy couldn't help asking. If she were younger, or they were older, these three might hold some appeal. There was an honesty that lurked beneath their bravado.

"They call me Stallone 'cause like Rocky I never stop trying. On the field or off." He smiled a devilish grin.

Judy couldn't help answering it with her own. She turned to the middle of the group. "And you're?"

"Dan. I don't need a stupid nickname. My skills speak for themselves."

Keep laughed. "Yeah, he thinks he can handle a ball, while everyone knows I'm the one—"

"Who can handle a ball?" Judy asked dryly.

Keep paused, thought a moment and then laughed, joined by his friends. "This one's a keeper, O'Brien. You haven't told us your name, sweetie." He wrapped his arm over her shoulder.

"Judy, Judy Bently."

"*The* Judy?" Keep looked impressed.

"As in 'Punch and Judy in the morning?'" Dan asked.

She nodded. "Guilty as charged. Peter and I were just—"

"Going over some business for the show. So, if you'll all excuse us," Peter said.

Judy's eyes met his. Business for work?

He didn't want anyone to know they were dating. Why?

Because despite what he'd said, she was just another conquest. Another woman to date, then move on. If he kept it quiet, then it would be easier when it was over.

"Work, that's for business hours. Now is the time to play. Bet you play poker, don't you Jude?" Stallone grinned.

"I sure do." She turned and waved at Peter. "Shall we, gentlemen? See you at *work*, O'Brien."

He grabbed her arm. "Like hell."

Judy shook it off. "Like the boys here said, business is from nine to five, or in our case, it starts at four-thirty, but same difference. Right now isn't time to talk business, it's time for—"

"Poker," the three young men supplied. Keep kept his arm firmly slung across her shoulder. "Come on honey, we'll show you a good time."

"Like hell you will," Peter growled and grabbed at Judy's arm, but she pulled away.

"Sorry, Peter, but the guys here are right. This business meeting was a mistake, one I'm rectifying by leaving. I'll see you around."

She allowed herself to be led from the room. The whole idea of her and Peter had been absurd from the beginning. She was just another woman in a long line of women for him.

She slammed his apartment door shut. "Let's go, guys."

Dan and Stallone led the way, but Keep held her back. "We didn't interrupt business, did we?"

"Of course you did. What else could it have been?

"Oh, you've got it bad, don't you?" The knowing smile he flashed was far too mature for someone his age.

"Got what?"

"Got it. The big *IT*, all capital letters. You've fallen and you've fallen hard."

She shook her head. "You couldn't be more wrong. Peter said it himself, we work together. That was all just business."

"That's what he said, but I don't think I believe it."

"Believe it or not, it doesn't matter. I'm here and he's not. So, let's play some poker. I was the quiet type in college, but back in high school we used to play a lot on long bus rides to games."

Keep led her down the hall. "Nose-in-a-book college sort?"

"Nose in lots of books. Plus I wasn't the type guys took to things like this."

"What type is that?"

"The kind guys drool over." There she'd said it. It wasn't exactly a revelation to either of them.

"Judy, I'd like to show you just how much a guy

could drool, given the chance, but O'Brien wouldn't appreciate it."

"O'Brien can bite me."

It was such an un-Judy-like thing to say, and yet, it was empowering. Peter O'Brien was used to women adoring him. He'd said it himself, she'd never joined the masses. That was her mistake, getting on that Punch bandwagon. Well, she was climbing back off.

He thought he liked that she didn't fawn all over him? Well, she'd show him how absolutely notfawning she could be.

The boys led her to a shabby apartment with a card table as the focal part of their decor.

She took a seat. "Let's play."

The boys were about to sit when the door opened and Peter stormed in. "Let's go, Jude."

She shook her head. "The boys want to play poker. Don't you, boys? All you want to do is talk business."

His eyes narrowed as he moved toward her. "Oh, yeah, we have business to discuss."

Judy might be funny, but she wasn't dumb. She backed up, keeping as much distance between them as possible. "Well, save it for work. Tonight I want some fun."

"We'll discuss fun after we're done discussing business. Now, put down the cards."

"Sorry, partner. I'm keeping the cards and getting rid of the man." She shuffled the deck. "This room ain't big enough for the both of us. So why don't you mosey along now, pardn'r?"

Peter sensed his moment and dove in for the kill. He grabbed Judy from her chair.

"Put me down, Peter. You'll break your back."

"I don't think so," he said, holding onto her tighter. "Want to get the door for me Keep?"

"Sure thing."

"Hey, this is just like that movie. You know the one with the army guy?" Stallone said.

"*An Officer and a Gentleman*?" Keep said dryly as he opened the door.

"Yeah, that's the one."

"I think he was navy." Charlie began to hum the theme song.

The other two joined in. They followed the couple down the hall humming.

"Go home, guys, before I have to kick your butts," Peter growled.

"Touchy, touchy, touchy," Charlie said. "Must be love."

Still humming, the boys started back down the hall. Keep hollered just before entering his apartment. "You just give me a call when O'Brien moves on to greener pastures, okay Jude?"

"I'll call you tomorrow then," she hollered back. "We all know that's about the lifespan of any of Peter's romantic interests."

Peter only squeezed tighter.

"Put me down, Peter."

He slammed the apartment door and moved through the living room. "In a second."

He tossed her on the couch and sat next to her—right next to her.

"Oh, no. You said we were here talking *business*. You can sit over there."

He wrapped his arms around her. He liked how it felt when he held her. Actually, there wasn't much about Judy Bently he didn't like, except maybe this little fit of irrationality she was displaying.

"You can't think we're going to—"

He nodded. "Oh yes, I can. I know we are. Kissing you is quite addictive."

She tried to break free, but Peter wasn't letting go. "Let me go, you loser! You told them I was here on business. Well, this type of business is what gets men in trouble! Go call one of your sex kittens, because I'm not interested!"

"Yes, you are. Is that what got you so mad? That I said we were talking about business?"

"I'm not mad."

"Oh, ho, ho. You're a liar as well. You're beyond mad. You're absolutely livid."

"Let me go, Peter."

"I just said that because I didn't think you really wanted the world to know we were seeing each other. I mean, if things don't work out, it could make work awkward."

"So you thought you'd be discreet and make things easier on us both when it was over?"

He nodded, relieved that she understood. He'd had one disastrous office romance and had never intended to take a chance on another one, but he couldn't stop himself. He wanted Judy enough to take a chance, but taking a chance didn't mean they couldn't be discreet.

"Because, of course, whatever we have will fizzle out and end, just like all your other relationships—and I use that term loosely because a few dates with a woman doesn't constitute a real relationship. That requires putting yourself on the line and taking a chance. But despite all your talk, you're not going to really do that. So we'll meet on the down-low. Here, or at my place after work, and no one would be the wiser?"

Another minute nod, as if he sensed the danger in her line of reasoning.

"Of course, we couldn't go out. Someone might see us."

"Right, that's what I thought."

"That's why you picked Waves, a secluded little restaurant, not because it was romantic, but because you wanted to hide me away."

"Come on, Jude." Peter had a feeling he had dug a hole, but he wasn't quite sure how it happened or how to get out of it.

She made a dive for freedom, but Peter caught her

and hauled her back to his side. "You want me. I want you. We're two adults, and we work together. I don't see why we can't have a relationship without broadcasting it throughout town."

"I'm sure you don't." She kicked him, but he held tight. "Let me go."

"Fine. You kiss me, and then tell me you don't want me, and I'll let you go."

"Fine." She leaned forward and planted a chaste kiss on his cheek. "There. I don't want you."

He grabbed her then and kissed her the way she was meant to be kissed, the way he'd been longing to kiss her. He wasn't sure just what had changed or when, but he knew he wanted Judy Bently in a way he'd never wanted any woman. Despite the very real reasons to avoid getting involved with her, he couldn't stop. He kissed her with all the pent-up longing and frustration he possessed, and then he kissed her some more.

"Peter, I don't want you," Judy whispered.

"Liar."

Chapter Eight

Kissing Peter was probably the biggest mistake Judy had ever made. Even bigger than kissing Stockly Camper in third grade. The little rat had told Mrs. Shefler's entire class that Beanpole had kissed him, and added *yuck* for emphasis.

If Peter said, "*Yuck*," Judy wouldn't be merely embarrassed, as she'd been in third grade. She'd be devastated.

But there was no *yuck* in Peter's passion-darkened eyes. Judy almost wished there were.

"Peter, you were right about everything. Taking our relationship to a new level is stupid. We work together. And, I've watched how your relationships all end. I don't want to be one of your casualties. For a few aberrant minutes I thought we could take a chance. But I've come to my senses. I think it's best I just say goodbye now, and leave with whatever dignity I can scrape together."

"That's really what you want? After that kiss, you're going to lie to me and say you want to go?"

"I'm not going to lie to you, Peter. I want you. But, I don't want you for just a night, or even a week. I'm greedy. I want it all. And *all* is the one thing you've never been able to give a woman."

"And if you can't have it all you don't want any?"

"Like I said, we both knew this was a mistake right from that first dance. You'll be over the disappointment tomorrow."

But Judy knew that she'd never recover. She didn't just want Peter, and what she felt wasn't some schoolgirl crush. She loved him. And because she loved him, she had to leave now. "Goodbye, Peter."

Feeling as if she was leaving behind the better part of her heart, Judy called a cab and left.

Peter knew he should say something.

Damning himself for being a coward, he let her call for a cab.

A gentleman would have offered to drive her home. Peter had never claimed to be a gentleman.

And he didn't have the faintest idea what to do with Judy. If they didn't work together, he wouldn't hesitate to pursue her. He'd hoped dating her would relieve whatever was buzzing between them.

He did a quick internal examination.

No. He didn't feel the least bit relieved. He wasn't sure what he felt, but "scared" was the first word that came to mind.

Peter heard the door shut softly.

Judy was gone.

A rush of something threatened to override even his fear. Peter wasn't sure just what it was. The fear was still there, but it was overshadowed by a feeling of loss.

That's what it was.

Loss.

Judy walked out of his arms, out of his house, and suddenly there was a hole where none had ever existed before.

He walked through the dark living room to the window and stared at the dark night.

He thought of the way Judy smelled, the way she felt in his arms. Nothing had changed. She was still Judy, and he was still Peter. "Punch and Judy in the morning." They still worked together. Nothing had changed, and yet, everything had changed.

Unreasonable anger surged through his body. She'd left him. She'd kissed him, and looked at him with those beautiful blue eyes, and then decided it was time to go.

How could she leave him like that? He was always the one to leave, and he'd always gone with a sense of relief.

But there was no relief present in the warring emotions that were raging through him. That had never happened before. Women came and went, and Peter O'Brien never batted an eye. But with Judy it was different.

She was different, and when he was with her, he was different as well.

Peter wasn't quite sure what to make of that difference, but he knew he wasn't ready to let Judy walk away from what was between them. It was going to be sticky, convincing her to see him as more than a co-worker. And, for the first time in a lot of years, Peter didn't feel the slightest urge to walk away when a relationship got sticky.

Judy sat on a stool, watching the coffee brew the next morning. She was still in her pajamas, a pair of cut-off sweats and a t-shirt from her high school basketball days.

She ran her fingers through her tangled hair. If only straightening out her tangled thoughts were as easy as raking the knots from her hair.

Last night had probably been one of the biggest mistakes she'd ever made. How could she have imagined she could rid Peter from her system and then things could go back to normal again?

Going on a date with him was a horrid mistake. And kissing him? Well, that was beyond mistaken.

But, oh, what a mistake it was! It had been a gloriously foolish blunder. Peter, being Peter, would never be able to return her feelings, but for those passion-filled moments in his arms, she could pretend.

She could pretend that after they'd kissed, he'd wrapped his arms around her and whispered, "I love you."

And in that dream, she would have of course whispered back, "I love you too."

But of course the words wouldn't have been enough. She needed bigger words to contain the wealth of what she felt for Peter.

She loved him.

"Darn," she muttered.

She could pretend all she wanted, but the reality of Peter was, he'd never say the words, and if she kept pretending he might one day return her feelings, she'd only get her heart broken.

Pretend. That's all she'd ever have with Peter. She could pretend that the relationship was going to keep growing, keep progressing, she could even pretend that someday Peter would care for her with the same intensity that she cared for him. But, all that pretending wouldn't get her anywhere in the end.

No, Judy wasn't the type to live in a fantasy world, at least not for long. She knew that her fantasies were just pipe-dreams. And now she was left to put her glorious mistake behind her. Somehow, she had to get her relationship with Peter back on a professional level.

Maybe they could manage the friendship thing.

He'd done it with Belinda.

Actually, he had a long line of women he had dated who were now friends. From his point of view, it wouldn't be hard to separate last night, their one beautiful almost-fling, from work and friendship.

Judy could manage it too. She'd have to. She'd pretend nothing had changed. She'd go to work Monday with a smile pasted on her face. She'd act outraged when he did his numerous Punch-ish things on air. She'd never let on that she was hopelessly, head-over-heels, in love with him.

The coffee finished perking—had finished perking somewhere in the middle of her ruminations, Judy realized.

With a small shake of her head, she jumped off the stool, and poured an oversized mug full of her black ambrosia.

Judy was a woman who functioned better with some concrete plan, and now she had one, such as it was.

She would smile and pretend nothing had changed. She would never let Peter know how much she cared. And when he started dating other women—and he was bound to start dating other women—she would just keep on smiling, even if it killed her.

She'd start trying to excise Peter O'Brien from her heart this morning. First step was a shower. A long, hot shower to wash the feel of Peter O'Brien from her body, from her soul.

Coffee in hand, she trudged toward the bathroom. The knock on the door stopped her in her tracks. Who on earth would be at her door before eight on a Saturday? She peeked through the front window.

Peter. Who else?

It was time to begin pretending.

She opened the door. "What?"

He pushed past her, and let himself into her kitchen. He stood in the center, turned a small circle and examined the room. "It looks like you."

"You're saying my kitchen is rumpled and in need of a shower?"

"I'm saying, it looks comfortable and lived in."

Judy had no idea if that was a compliment or an insult, so she just ignored it and followed Peter as he made a bee line for the coffee maker. He started rummaging through the cupboard over it.

"Looking for a mug?" She opened the appropriate door and allowed him to choose his own.

He poured the coffee and took a tentative sip. "Too weak."

"I know. The spoon doesn't stand by itself."

She'd learned in basketball that sometimes the best defense was a good offense. She needed all the defenses she could get. "Since I'm sure you didn't come over here this early to discuss my inability to make coffee to your liking, maybe you should tell me what you want. I have to take a shower."

"Do you need help?" He grinned mischievously.

Judy's heart beat double-time, but she ignored it.

Friends. They were friends.

Colleagues.

"I've managed to shower on my own all these years. I think I can handle one more morning. Did you need something, Peter?"

"Just this." He set his mug down, reached for hers, and placed it by his.

"Peter." She could see what he was going to do, it was there in his eyes. She should avoid it.

She had a plan.

They were going to be just friends. Kissing him could lead to other things, and those things would endanger her fragile hold on friendship. She might slip up, and he'd find out how she felt. She was prepared to stand losing him, even though she'd just found him, but she couldn't bear the thought of his pity.

"No. We're back to being just colleagues. Our one and only date was a disaster. Chalk it up to Ethan and Mary's wedding. Like you said, weddings do strange things to women. Thinking we had a chance at anything was just an aberration. I'm over it."

She glanced at the kitchen clock. "I'm sorry. I've got to run, or I'm going to be late."

She hadn't really expected a protest on his part,

but still, it annoyed her that he didn't try to make at least a token *are you sure?* All he said was, "Late?"

"The Babes have a game today. I'm meeting them at the gym at eight-thirty for a nine o'clock game."

Peter glanced at the clock. "You'll never be ready in time."

"Watch me." Despite all her good intentions, Judy couldn't resist one last taste. She kissed him, hard and fast—it was the last time she'd indulge herself— then ran toward the bathroom.

"You know where the door is," she shouted over her shoulder.

Peter watched Judy fly down the hall.

Yeah, he knew where the door was, but he didn't plan on using it, at least not until Judy left for her game. He'd managed one grade-school game, he figured another wouldn't kill him.

Seeing him again might keep those conniving mothers from trying to fix Judy up again. She was definitely not on the market, even if she didn't know it yet. She was going to learn.

While he worked on it, he'd just have to hang around and see to it that she got used to having him be a part of her life. If that meant watching her team slaughter his favorite sport, well so be it.

He poured another mug of coffee and glanced at the clock. There was no way she was going to be ready in time.

Women took hours to get put together in the morning. Maybe he should holler and ask if there was someone he should call?

At that moment, Judy walked into the kitchen.

"You're ready?"

"I said, I had to be out of here. Did you think I was kidding?" She stared at him a moment. "And why are you still here?"

"I don't have anything better to do, so I thought I'd tag alone."

"Peter, you don't have to. Last night, the date was nice, and afterward was a mistake we avoided. We're friends we decided, but I didn't take it as a sign that we were going to be tied at the hips. I appreciate the concern."

She smiled and patted his cheek. "But, run along and do whatever it is you do on Saturdays."

She patted his cheek as if he was some little boy she needed to placate. Peter's smile felt brittle on his face. "I don't have any plans. Is there a reason you don't want me at your game?"

Maybe one of those moms had fixed her up and she didn't want him messing with her plans. The thought made Peter's blood run cold, then hot.

She shook her head, sending her damp curls springing out of her ponytail. "No, no reason. I just didn't want you to feel obligated. I can't imagine watching a bunch of pre-adolescents is your idea of how to spend a weekend."

"I can't think of anything I'd rather do." The truth of the matter was that anything he could do with Judy was appealing. "Ready?"

Judy glanced over her shoulder. He was sitting in the middle of the Babes' parents, as if he belonged there.

A king surrounded by his loyal subjects.

Men. She just didn't understand them. Peter should be doing anything he could to put distance between them, not tagging after her.

"Coach?"

She pulled her gaze from Peter, and forced herself to get her mind on the game they were about to play. "Sorry."

She looked at ten faces staring at her expectantly, waiting for her to say something brilliant. Judy couldn't think of a single even semi-brilliant thing to say.

"Coach?" Abbey asked.

"What?"

"They're going to kill us, aren't they?"

"Yeah, that Leah can really handle the ball, and Emily is the best shot in the league—"

Judy interrupted their pessimistic grumbles. "The only people who can beat us today is ourselves, and we're not going to let that happen. Are we?"

"No!" came a roar that only ten pre-teens could make.

"How are we supposed to tell the twins apart?" Jess Jacobs asked.

"Yeah, I'm in class and Andrea and Erin say not even their mom can tell them apart." Kate glanced at the five girls gathering in the center of the floor.

"I'll bet they don't wear numbers at home."

Judy's words had their desired affect; ten girls grinned.

"Jess, Misty, Sarah, Amanda and Claire. You're up. The three Kates, Abbey and Mandy, you'll go up next. Come on girls, let's show the Wesleyville Warriors what we're made of."

Five cheering girls took the floor, and Judy took her seat by the other five on the bench. She sensed Peter in the bleachers, but she didn't turn. She didn't want him to think she cared. He obviously didn't need any encouragement.

She was suddenly brought back to the game with a bang as Kate made a three point shot. "Way to go, Kate!" She smiled. Peter or no Peter, this was going to be a wonderful day.

Wonderful day.

Ha.

Peter was sure he'd had a worse time, but he couldn't think of when. Because he'd blocked her car in the driveway, Judy had reluctantly agreed to ride with him. She was distant and impersonal. He wasn't quite sure how to approach her. It was almost as if she didn't want anything more to do with him.

But that couldn't be.

He didn't think he was conceited thinking that way. Women had always wanted him. He was smart enough to realize it was just for his looks. After that one disastrous near miss, that suited him just fine, but somewhere along the line it had grown old. He wanted someone who wanted him for who he was. Someone who saw the real him.

Judy did see him. She didn't take his crap at work. She liked him because of, or maybe in spite of, who he was.

She was different. Rather than falling all over him, she was doing her best to put as much distance between them as she could. The entire ride to the game had consisted of listening to the radio. Every time he tried to say something, she just cranked the radio a little louder.

He didn't know what to do with her.

"See, I told you it was him." Herb's wife and her cronies filled the bleacher seats beside him. "I knew you couldn't stay away."

"Oh?" A half dozen eyes were gazing at him. Peter shifted nervously in his seat.

"Oh yes," cooed Herb's wife, the obvious leader of the group. "We could see the sparks flying between you and our Judy."

"I see." He turned his attention to the game, hoping they'd take the hint.

They didn't.

"Are you planning a spring wedding?"

"On the air, like Mary and Ethan's?"

"Oh, that was so romantic. And to think, their romance was the start of yours."

"Judy's a lucky woman."

Herb's wife shut them all up with a look. "Peter's a lucky man."

"Thanks, I think." He stood. "It's been nice talking to you all again, but I promised Judy I'd give her a hand." Without another word, he beat a hasty retreat.

He motioned for the girls to make some room on the bleacher, and thankfully sank onto the seat next to Judy.

She glanced and frowned. "Peter?"

"Please, smile and look happy to see me."

"Why?"

"The mother brigade. They found me, even though I purposely sat way over in the other corner. They found me and surrounded me. They scare me, Jude. Be a pal and play along. I told them I promised to help coach. I'll be your assistant. I'll fill water bottles, tape ankles and do any other menial task you can think of, only don't send me back to *them*."

She shrugged. "Okay."

*　　*　　*

What was he up to? Judy studied Peter. He didn't seem to notice. He was too wrapped up in the game.

Wrapped up in the game? Huh. No. He was pretending to be wrapped up in the game. Peter wasn't the type of man who became engrossed in a middle school game.

"Peter—" She started, then interrupted herself by shouting, "Great pick, Jess."

"Peter—"

"Grab the rebound, Katie," he hollered. When the girl did just that, he clapped and shouted, "That's it."

"Peter, I want to know what you think you're doing."

"Watching the game, Jude. What are you doing? It seems I'm doing more coaching than—did you see that?"

Judy hated to admit she hadn't. "I—"

"Abbey just snapped that ball out of the tall girl's hands. Who said height was everything?"

"Not me, certainly. I hate being tall. Now, about the game—"

"You'd better get your mind on it. We're winning, but call a play, Coach. They're stuck."

"Phantom," Judy called.

"Phantom?"

"Now you see her, now you don't."

"Sort of like you last night," he said.

"Peter, shut up."

"I'm shutting. Now, watch your game and coach your team."

How on earth was she supposed to think, much less coach, with him sitting right next to her? His thighs brushed hers. Judy found her attention wasn't on team sports; she was fantasizing about a good game of one-on-one.

Oh, for pete's sake, she couldn't go on thinking about him like this. She needed space, but Peter wouldn't give it to her. He was here crowding her, forcing her to face what they'd almost done last night.

"Call a play, Abbey."

"Slow it down," Peter whispered to Judy.

"I can coach my team."

"So coach and stop daydreaming about me."

"You conceited a—"

"Uh, uh, uh. Young ears and all that," he whispered. Louder, he added. "Conceited assistant? Of course I am. Everyone knows Judy Bently doesn't settle for second best, so of course I'm feeling conceited today."

"Shut up, Peter."

The buzzer sounded. Judy looked up at the clock, amazed the game had ended. "See what you did?" she hissed.

"What?"

"Broke my concentration."

Judy couldn't decide who she was angrier with,

Peter, or herself. She didn't want him to affect her this way. She didn't want him acting so out of character. She'd been his partner long enough to realize that this wasn't normal. He dated women, yes. But pursue them? Never. Peter was the one who was pursued.

So what was he doing here?

Judy couldn't figure it out.

"Coach, Coach, we won!" The girls came running off the floor and thoughts of Peter faded as Judy congratulated them and followed them in line, shaking the other team's hands.

"Good game. Good game," she chanted along with the girls. She could almost feel Peter's eyes burning holes into her back.

Well, let him. She didn't care. She didn't want anything more to do with him. She'd decided they'd be friends, like he was with Belinda, and then he shows up acting all strange.

She trailed after the girls into the locker room.

"Great game, girls. There's just one more, the big game against the Waterford Generals next weekend and then our season's done." She went on to talk about problems and successes in the game . . . at least as much of it as she'd seen. "We'll be practicing Tuesday and Thursday. Any questions?"

"Are we still going for ice cream?" Katie asked.

Ice cream with a team full of pre-teens. If that didn't get rid of Peter, nothing would.

Judy couldn't help but smile. "Sure are."

Oh, yeah, they were going for ice cream and she was going to shake Peter O'Brien. The day was suddenly looking brighter.

The girls dressed and they went out in mass to greet the parents, waiting for them in a huddle. Peter was there too. Judy walked over to him, still grinning.

"Peter, if you drop me off at my house, I can drive myself. The team is going out for ice cream, and I'm sure you have better things to do today than sit around and—"

"Nope." Dark eyes were sparkling with mischief.

"Nope what?" Judy asked suspiciously. Peter looked way too happy for her to feel comfortable.

"No, I don't have anything better to do. And, yes, I love ice cream." He gave her a brazen grin and then to the girls. "So, where are we going?"

"You're going too?" Jess Jacobs looked as if she'd received a delicious candy and wanted to savor the taste.

"Of course I'm going. I'm the new assistant coach, aren't I?"

"You are," came his chorus of converts.

There he went, charming every female between the ages of ten and ninety. If there were any babies, he'd probably charm them as well. The man was incorrigible. He'd never settle down for just one woman.

He'd never settle down for just you, an inner little voice whispered.

Judy followed the excited girls and their parents out of the gym, trying to harden her heart against the man who was sure to break it.

Chapter Nine

Though the ice cream with the girls didn't scare Peter off, Judy was sure the grocery store would. But he tagged along, acting as if shopping for melons was the highlight of his life.

"Not that one." He grabbed the cantaloupe from her hand.

"Why not?"

He sniffed it, then put it back in the pile. "It's not ripe."

He hefted its neighbor and smelled it. "Now, this one will be sweet and juicy. Just what you want in a melon and in a—"

She cut him off. "It's fine, put it in the cart."

She'd hope to bore him to death with her shopping, but instead, he seemed to revel in it.

156

"No, no, not that one. It's bigger, so you think you're saving, but look," he pointed at the little white tags under the coffee. "See, it gives the actual price, and then what it costs per pound. See, two smaller containers are actually cheaper."

"Peter, I just want some coffee. I don't want to turn every purchase into a debate."

"I'm not debating anything. Two is cheaper than one in this case."

"Fine. Put the two in the cart," she grumbled.

"What's next?"

"Tea. I want green tea. Go ahead and pick whichever one whistles your kettle." She watched him study the three brands that were available as if lives depended on the decision he reached.

It was kind of . . . cute.

Not that she going to tell him that. She was trying to get rid of him, after all, not encourage him.

"Here." He held a box aloft. "This is the best deal."

Despite her good intentions, Judy couldn't help but chuckle. "I never imagined you were such a tightwad."

"I'm not a tightwad, I'm just frugal."

Her eyes narrowed. "You clip coupons, don't you?"

"It's free money. I can't believe you don't. I'd have thought careful, sensible Judy Bently would worry about such things."

Judy's moment of humor faded. Of course he thought she would clip coupons. Frugal, dependable, sensible—that's how he saw her.

Judy named her items and let him pick them out for the rest of the shopping. The fun had evaporated. Whatever had him pursuing her like this wouldn't last. It was probably just the novelty of having a woman say no.

Groceries were put away, the laundry was done and put away as well, Judy had scrubbed toilets and floors, vacuumed and dusted, and was still waiting for the moment Peter got tired and left. But he didn't.

He'd eaten cold cut sandwiches for lunch with no complaint. He'd lifted furniture for her. He'd acted as if it didn't matter what they did—as if he just wanted to be with her. But, Judy wasn't buying it.

"Come on. Even you can't find another job that needs doing in this house." Peter was lounging at the kitchen table, as Judy finished putting the last of the dishes in the dishwasher.

"I . . ." Judy racked her brain for another job, but couldn't think of one.

She needed something to do, something to keep her busy if she was going to be forced to spend any more time with Peter. "Dinner. I have to start dinner."

"No you don't," he said.

"Yes, I do, unless those sandwiches filled you up." She wiped the counter, which didn't really need to be wiped.

Peter was out of his chair and reached her in a step. He spun her around. "We're going out."

"No. Being hidden in some out-of-the-way bistro so no one sees you with me isn't really all that good for my digestion."

She was pushing him and knew it. She just hoped if she pushed hard enough, she'd push him out of her home and out of her life. She'd decided they were going to keep their relationship professional, but it was hard when his very-kissable lips were just inches from hers.

"Damn it, Judy. Why are you making things so hard today? If I didn't want to be seen with you, would I have gone to that game, to the ice cream store, to the grocery store?"

"I don't know. I don't understand what's going on. We worked together for an entire year, no problems at all. But ever since that 'Pickup Lines' contest, things have been odd."

"Is it so odd, so hard to believe, that I just wanted to spend a day with you?" He loosened his grip on her shoulders, but didn't let go.

"Yes," she whispered. "I've seen the women come and go in your life. I know how things are supposed to happen. You date them a few times—a dinner here, a movie there—and then it's over. Two weeks later you don't remember their names. They call, you gently put them off until they get the picture. You don't spend entire days with them, you don't chase them to teenaged basketball games. You don't choose their cantaloupe. So, yes, I'm confused. I don't understand what's going on."

"Jude, I . . ." he paused, as if trying to piece together the right words.

Judy held her breath, not sure what she wanted him to say.

"I wanted to spend the day with you. Basketball, cantaloupes, it didn't matter. I just wanted to be with you, just like I want to go to dinner with you now. What's so hard to understand?"

"You." She pushed against his chest, but Peter didn't move. "You're so hard to understand."

"So stop trying so hard and just enjoy it. Come to dinner with me. We'll go walk along the beach and watch the sunset. Just be with me."

She should say no. She should kick him out and get on with her life. She should do just about anything other than going out to dinner with Peter O'Brien and giving him the chance to crawl deeper into her heart. Despite all the things she should have said, should have done, Judy found herself saying, "Okay."

Monday mornings—whoever invented them was a masochist.

Judy had always firmly believed that, especially at five o'clock on a Monday morning.

She sipped her coffee and tried to avoid looking at

Peter. She'd finally rid herself of him Saturday night. She'd held hopes that Saturday was it.

Even when he showed up Sunday morning, she thought she could shake him by going to church, but he'd simply insisted he'd like nothing better than to attend service with her.

She'd tried to shake him Sunday afternoon when she had volunteered to load groceries for the food pantry. He'd rolled up his sleeves and pitched in, endearing himself to core members of the congregation.

She'd given up by dinner. Peter had pitched in, helping prepare the meal as if he'd always cooked in her kitchen. He hadn't even complained when she turned on an old Tracy and Hepburn movie.

No, he hadn't complained, and he hadn't touched her again. Judy should have been relieved, but his physical distance just made her aware of how emotionally close he was coming.

Relief? Not a bit of it. Each passing minute with Peter left her more terrified.

Finally, after dinner, he'd simply left on his own. No fights, no ploys.

"Work tomorrow," he'd explained.

As she hid behind the curtain and watched his headlights recede, Judy was sure she'd finally chased him off for good. And she'd been pleased—darned pleased.

She kept reassuring herself about how pleased she

was all night long as she tossed and turned. Her bout of insomnia had absolutely nothing to do with Peter's strange behavior, or the fact that every time she shut her eyes, she could see him smiling at her. She could feel him touching her, kissing her.

No, her sleepless night had nothing to do with Peter.

She took another sip of coffee and glanced in his direction. He was pouring brown sludge from his thermos. He glanced up and his eyes met hers . . . and held hers.

"You look tired."

Judy started to reply, but realized she'd been holding her breath. She exhaled, then inhaled deeply and opted to just shrug. Let him make of it what he would.

"We're on in ten," he said.

She adjusted her headset and jiggled the mike. "Good morning. This is Judy Bently—"

"—and Punch O'Brien. Punch and Judy in the morning here at your favorite radio station, WLVH Lovehandles, where love is more than just a song."

He cued Judy.

"It's already seventy degrees here in Erie at 5:03."

"And it looks like it's going to get hotter—much hotter. So, in the spirit of the weather, here's a song." He punched the button and "In the Heat of the Night," filled the studio's speakers before he muted them.

"That's not on our log." Judy took another gulp of her coffee, then started fidgeting with tapes for the upcoming hour.

Peter's hands covered hers, stilling them. "Is this awkwardness going to be a permanent fixture of the show?"

She pulled her hands from his and just barely resisted wiping them on her sweats. She couldn't afford to let him see how much he affected her. "I don't know what you're talking about."

Peter's left eyebrow rose, but he said nothing.

"I hate it when you do that. You look like Spock from Star Trek."

She busied herself stacking jewel cases. She'd do anything to keep from looking at Peter. Though it was as scenic as viewing Lake Erie at sunset, it was as dangerous, at least for Judy, as dining with the white Bengal tiger at the zoo.

"Spock would agree with me."

She glanced up, a fatal mistake. Peter chose that moment to smile, and any thoughts of Spock fled— any rational thought soon followed. "Spock would agree with what?"

"That your behavior isn't logical."

"I don't know what you mean." Even Spock wouldn't expect her to be logical when Peter was smiling.

"And lying to yourself isn't logical either."

Thoughts of smiles and jewel cases evaporated as

anger welled up in Judy's chest. She welcomed the feeling. Anger was preferable to mooning over a man she could never have. "How dare you!"

"How dare I what? Care about you? I don't know myself. I sure as hell don't want to." He drained his cup of the thick sludge he called coffee and slammed the mug onto the counter. "We work together, and this morning is one of the prime reasons why colleagues should never date.

"We're not dating," Judy gritted out.

"And what would you call this weekend?"

That killer Peter O'Brien smile was back again, but this time it didn't inspire lust-filled thoughts; it just deepened Judy's anger.

He was mocking her. He was so used to women falling over themselves for a hint of that smile. Well, Judy would be damned if she was going to fall under its warm spell again. "You're being perverse."

"And when we kissed?"

Judy held onto her anger, unwilling to let her feelings about Peter's kisses melt her, like so many of his other women. "I'd call it an aberration for me, normal behavior for you."

"Oh, you think so?"

"I know so. Peter, I don't know what's going on. The basketball games, the dinner, and yesterday? Jeesh, Peter, you spent your weekend shopping, cleaning, and going to church. You might think you want me, but eventually you'll get tired of me, just like all the others. I know how the game is played."

"You don't know a thing." This time there was no smile evident on Peter's face. He looked angry, as angry as Judy felt. "You don't know a thing," he repeated, "not a thing. But, you're going to learn."

"Peter—"

"We're on in twenty. Just sit down and shut up, Jude. You're really getting me mad now."

"I'm not trying to." Maybe she was trying, but having Peter mad, and being mad at Peter, were both preferable to the warm mushy feeling he'd been evoking in her lately. "I just want to be honest about who we are and where this is going."

"It's going—"

She cued him. "Hi, you're on with Punch and Judy in the morning. It's six after five and—"

Peter jumped in. "—we have a question for the day. What is it women want from men? I can't figure them out. I'm seeing this beautiful, intelligent, talented woman, and I'm trying to build a real relationship, but she just wants me on a physical level. All she seems to see is a pretty face. Women say they want men who listen, who are caring, but I've found women really just want one thing, and once they have it, it's hasta la vista, baby."

"Peter."

He glared at her. "So, if any of you ladies have an

idea what I can do to show this lady that I'd like more than just a physical relationship, more than just stolen kisses in the parking lot of her life, give me a call."

Judy tossed her headset down on the counter. "What do you think you're doing?"

"Trying to understand you." Peter wasn't sure how he was going to understand Judy, when he hardly understood himself.

"What's to understand? Peter, I know the score. I've watched you date hundreds of women."

"I'm flattered by the number, but I don't think there were quite that many." And, recently, the women he'd dated were just faint memories. It was as if they ceased to exist when he saw Judy Bently, really saw her.

Peter glanced across the counter at the woman he'd worked with for a year, but never really *seen* until the "Pickup Lines" contest.

Her lake blue eyes were flashing with anger.

Peter, in a rare flash of insight, knew she was using that anger to keep a wall between them—a wall he was determined to tear down.

"There were enough women for me to know the rules," she said. "I went into things with my eyes wide open. Date. Break up. Be friends. But you're changing the rules, and I don't understand these new ones."

"I guess I'll just have to try and explain them better. But right now, I think we'd better answer the phones." The lights indicating calls were flashing like crazy.

"Hi. Who's this?" he asked.

"This is Milly. I think any woman would be a fool not to see what a good thing she has with you."

"I happen to agree." Peter grinned as Judy slammed CD jewel cases into their slots. "Do you have any suggestions?"

"Mutual interests. A girl likes a man who likes at least some of the things she does."

"Mutual interests. Good idea, Milly. Thanks for calling."

He punched button for another line. "WLVH. Good morning. Who is this?"

"This is Shirley. And I've got a suggestion for your woman problems. You need to woo her. In my day, couples courted. Hand holding. Flowers. Candy. Movies. Maybe rather than just jumping the gun and taking the relationship to a physical level, you need to do some old-fashioned courting. Show her how special she is."

"Thanks, Shirley." Courting Judy. Peter smiled. Shirley had a better idea than she knew.

"WLVH Lovehandles," he said, a plan forming in his mind.

"Hi, Peter. This is Darla. You need to talk to her. Let her know how you feel. Let everyone know how you feel. Women like to hear the words."

"Thanks, Darla. I'll give it a try."

Mutual interests. Flowers. Courting. The words women wanted to hear.

Well, men wanted to hear those words too.

"We're on in a minute," Judy said.

Peter fiddled with the tape machine as the clock clicked down, splicing together pieces of his calls, thinking about them in relationship to Judy. He wasn't quite sure when she'd become such an important part of his life, but she had.

Judy cued him and began, "It's quarter after and—"

Peter cut her off. "I've received some calls. Here's a few clips from Milly, Shirley and Darla. "Mutual interests . . . You need to woo her. In my day, couples courted. Hand holding. Flowers. Candy. Movies. Maybe rather than just jumping the gun, you need to do some old-fashioned courting. Show her how special she is . . . You need to talk to her. Let her know how you feel. Let everyone know how you feel. Women like to hear the words."

"Thanks to Milly, Shirley and Darla. You've given me an idea." An idea about how to woo a beautiful, slightly hostile, co-worker.

Judy watched Peter's smile, and a feeling of dread built in her chest. Whatever his idea was, she didn't think she was going to like it.

His chestnut eyes held her gaze a moment, and his smile grew broader.

No, she didn't think she was going to like this idea at all.

She didn't know what to make of him and she certainly didn't understand the game he was playing. And it certainly was a game. Peter wasn't the type to pursue a woman—women pursued him. So what was with this survey and all this talk about relationships? The only relationships Peter built were short-lived at best.

Courting?

The day Peter O'Brien courted any woman would be . . . *Absurd*, came to mind. Thinking Peter would ever be interested enough in any woman—including Judy—to court her was absolutely the most absurd thing she'd ever heard.

The Waterford Generals filed into the gym on Saturday. Judy was relieved to have gotten through the week—the very strange, very uncomfortable week.

Peter acted anything but Peter-ish. He was almost congenial. Every day, after the show, he disappeared, and every evening, right before dinner, he showed up on her doorstep. They ate, they talked, and he left.

He left without touching her, without kissing her.

Judy should be glad. Maybe this . . . She tried to pin a word on what was going on between them. Infatuation, maybe? Maybe this infatuation was beginning to fade.

She should be pleased.

Judy glanced at her gorgeous co-host and assistant coach. Yes, she should be relieved, but she didn't feel a bit relieved.

"They're big, Coach," Katie F. said, pulling Judy from her worries.

Enough. She had a game to coach, and she wasn't going to let Peter's odd behavior distract her today.

"They look real big," Kate H. echoed.

"But we're going to beat them," Peter said.

He was still playing at assistant coach. Judy just wished he'd give it up, give up whatever game he was playing. Then she wouldn't have to stand next to him and wonder how long until his lips touched hers again.

"Coach?" Peter asked, interrupting her from her lurid fantasies.

Fantasies that she couldn't shake. They interrupted her work, interrupted her sleep, and obviously interrupted her coaching.

Well, she'd be darned if she was going to let the Generals beat the Babes just because she couldn't keep her mind off Peter O'Brien.

"Okay, girls, here's what we're going to do. We'll play man-to-man defense. Kate, you'll . . ."

Peter watched Judy outline her plans for the game. He studied her small movements, how the girls hung on her every word. Hell, he was hanging on them as well. Her every word, her every movement, captivated him.

Judy might not have been right about the numbers, but she was right about the fact he'd dated other women, a lot of women. But not one of them could hold a candle to Judy.

He'd been determined not to become too involved, convinced that no woman would ever see the real him. He almost laughed at the thought. It sounded like something off some talk-show psychology segment.

Pretty boys who want women to see beyond the facade. But as corny as it sounded, even to himself, Peter knew that's what he'd been looking for. And he'd found it in Judy Bently. He smiled as he watched her animated pre-game speech.

Not one of those other women had Judy's mixture of brashness and insecurity. Not one of them read him the riot act as effectively as she did. Not one of them made him feel as much, as deeply, as Judy did.

He loved her.

He wasn't quite sure when he'd realized he loved her. Maybe it was when she walked out of his apartment with the three college boys. Maybe it was the first time they kissed. Or maybe he'd always loved her and he'd only just awakened to the fact.

Peter O'Brien loved Judy Bently. Every time he

thought those words they struck him anew. He loved Judy.

Flowers. Courting. Words.

Today was the day. There was no more appropriate place to court a coach, than on a basketball court.

"Today is the day," he said to the team as Judy wound down.

Ten pair of eyes stared at him, ten smiles lit ten faces. "We're all going to be winners today, right?"

Winning.

That was the only option. Winning Judy. Making her understand she was different, she was special. Making her see that he loved her, and making her see she loved him too.

"Right," came the loud response.

"Now, go make your coaches look good."

"What was that all about?" Judy asked, eyeing Peter's strange expression.

"What?" he asked, all too innocent.

"You're up to something O'Brien." Her eyes narrowed. "I want to know what it is."

"We don't always get what we want, do we Jude? I mean, if we did, then I would have had you—"

"I want to know what you're up to."

"Guess you're just going to have to wait." He patted the bench next to him.

Judy sat, but continued to stare at him.

"You've got a game to coach, Coach. I suggest you do your job, and stop undressing me with your eyes."

He watched, delighted as she ruffled, and appeared to turn her attention to the girls.

"I'm not undressing you," she said, her eyes glued to the court.

Peter leaned close and whispered, "Only because we're in a gym, surrounded by people. If we were someplace private, undressing me would be your top priority."

Judy's eyes pinned his. "You're still incorrigible, O'Brien."

"And you're still hiding, Bently. But not for long."

With that parting cryptic statement, Peter's attention turned to the game. Judy tried to ignore the nagging feeling that something was going on and that she was somehow the only one out of the loop.

At the start of the second half, the Babes were ahead, but barely. Thirty-seven to thirty-three wasn't a comfortable lead, and Judy was so wrapped up in the game that Peter's strange behavior was all but forgotten. "Come on Mandy! Move your feet!" Judy yelled.

"Come on girls!" Peter echoed. He reached over and gripped Judy's knee. "Sarah, get the rebound!"

Judy tried to ignore his touch, just as she had tried to ignore his presence.

"Find your man!" she called.

"Have you found yours?" Peter asked softly.

"What?" She tore her eyes from the game and

glanced at her crazy partner and unwanted assistant coach.

"I said, have you found your man?"

Judy shook her head. "Not yet. But you know me, I just keep trying," she quipped.

"No joking, Jude. I need to know—"

Judy cut him off. "Not now, Peter. We've got a game to win."

She turned from him and focused her attention on the game, ignoring the man and his hand on her thigh.

Peter should have been insulted; instead, he smiled. Judy was running, but he was about to put a stop to that.

Chapter Ten

"We won!" Judy watched her team come in, but there was something subdued about them. "Girls, you won."

Ten girls smiled and called out, half-hearted, "Yeah, Coach," while all ten eyes were glued on Peter.

"Coach O'Brien. Didn't you mention a contest?" Katie asked.

"Contest?" Judy eyed her on-air partner and off-air thorn in her side. What was Peter up to?

"Don't you all occasionally have a foul shot contest?" Peter, the picture of innocence, asked her.

"Occasionally to raise money. Why? What's going on?" Judy asked. They'd won. Why wasn't anyone on the Babes' side of the gym cheering? "Girls?"

They all just stared at Peter.

"Is everyone ready?" he asked.

"Ready for what?" Judy asked, with mounting frustration. How dare he waltz into her gym, mess with her team and somehow dim their enthusiasm for ending a winning season!

She realized that the real outrage was, how dare he waltz into her life and throw it into upheaval!

Judy just wanted . . .

The truth of it was, Judy just wanted Peter, but she was intelligent enough to realize that was never going to happen, at least not long-term. He might have spent the last week with her, but it wouldn't last.

Peter smiled, got up, and walked to the center of the gym. "Ladies and gentlemen," he called to get their attention, but it didn't appear to be necessary. The entire gym, even the Generals, hung on his ever word.

"As most of you know, I'm Peter 'Punch' O'Brien from WLVH. Our slogan at the station is, 'WLVH Lovehandles, where love is more than just a song.' As some of you know, we ran a contest at the beginning of the summer, our 'Pickup Lines' contest. Watching Mary and Ethan, I started to realize something about myself, something I never imagined. I wanted what they had. And I did this brief look around at the women I'd dated, and realized none of them were what I wanted. None of them were who I wanted."

Abbey tossed him a ball. Standing at the foul line, he began to dribble it as he continued. "I started looking around and realized there was only one woman for me. She's beautiful, she's smart, and best of all, she doesn't want to admit it. She sees me as I really am and likes me anyway. I'm kind of hoping she's even learned to more than like me.

"Anyway, I decided to come up with my own contest. The ultimate foul shooting contest. Do you want to see if I can sink this shot?"

Cheers erupted from the crowd, but Judy couldn't tell if they were screaming for him to throw his foul shot, or for him to continue with what he was saying.

She knew which she'd be screaming for, if she were screaming. But the moment Peter began his strange soliloquy, she'd mysteriously lost the ability to speak, much less scream. She was rooted to the floor, her eyes glued to the man she loved more than words could say.

"The question is, what do I get if I make the shot? What's my prize for winning?"

"What do you want, Punch?" Hank's wife called from the bleachers.

"If I make the shot, maybe I should get to name my prize?"

The crowd's cheers were even louder this time.

"Okay, I make the shot, I name my prize and it's up to all of you to help me see to it I get it."

He set his feet on the foul line and lined the ball up with the basketball hoop. "I asked a question earlier this week on the air. What do women want?" Peter dropped the ball back to the floor.

"Mutual interests."

Bounce.

"Courting."

Bounce.

"The words."

Bounce.

The girls started cheering as Peter put the ball in the air. The audience grew silent as they watched the ball make a perfect arc and swoosh into the basket. The cheers went from wild to utter pandemonium.

Peter raised his hands and there was silence. "It's time for me to name my prize. Do you think I'd be accused of being . . . What's the word, Jude? Incorrigible? Do you think I'd be accused of being incorrigible if I said, for my prize, I wanted a woman? Not just any woman, a very special woman?"

"No!" the crowd called.

"When I asked what women wanted, Lovehandle's listeners told me. Court her. Well, what better place to court a woman who loves basketball than on the court?"

"And flowers," he said.

Katie F. tapped Judy on the shoulders and handed her a bouquet of daisies and yellow tea roses.

"And another listener assured me in order to claim the ultimate prize, a women needs to hear the words, she needs to know what a man is feeling."

Peter left the foul line, walked right up to Judy. He sandwiched her cheeks in his hands, forcing her eyes to meet his. "The words in this case would be, 'I love you, Judy Bently.' I've discovered that all those other women I dated were just my attempts to find you. And you were there, sharing a mike with me, all the time."

Jess Jacobs came forward and handed Peter a small black box. He flipped open the lid as he sank to his knees. "Judy, the words in this case would have to be, 'I love you. Will you marry me?' "

This was it. Judy oh-so-sensible Bently realized somewhere along the line she had totally lost her mind.

"What?" she managed to blurt out.

Louder, he repeated himself. "Judy Bently, will you marry the man who loves you?"

"Peter, I don't know what this game is, but, like I said, I don't like playing if I don't know the rules."

"The only rules are you have to love me back," he took her hand in his, "And you have to say you'll be my wife."

All along she'd tried to convince herself that things with Peter could never work out because she was plain old Beanpole Bently. That wasn't the truth. The truth was, she'd tried to convince herself that things could never work out with Peter because she was afraid.

Now, looking into the eyes of the man she loved, any remnants of fear melted. She loved him and, by some mysterious magic, he loved her too. Judy could see it in his eyes as he watched her, waiting for her answer. She saw his love, and she also saw nervousness. Peter O'Brien was as afraid as she was.

"Yes," she whispered. Feeling empowered, she repeated "Yes," louder.

Peter rose to his feet. "Yes?"

"Yes." As she walked into his open arms, a feeling of coming home swept over her. This is where she was meant to be. And at the moment, wrapped in Peter's arms and in his love, Beanpole Bently once and for all ceased to exist.

Peter tipped her head and smiled down at her. "Yes. Is that all you have to say?"

"What more could I say?" she asked.

"Men like to hear the words too, Jude. I need them."

"I love you, Peter. I've been in love with you since that first day we worked together."

"Why on earth didn't you say something sooner?" He kissed her and the crowd started cheering. "Why would you let me waste all that time?"

"Because I'm a woman who didn't believe in

fairytales until a certain man pointed out that if I looked in the mirror and truly saw myself, I could do anything. I looked and what I saw was you standing next to me."

"Say the words, Judy."

"I love you. I looked in the mirror through your eyes and I feel like I can do anything right now."

"And?"

"And one of those things I'll be doing is marrying you."

Ten little girls roared their approval, followed by all the basketball moms and the rest of the crowd.

Peter turned to the crowd and shouted, "WLVH Lovehandles is a place where love is more than just a song, and stay tuned, because we're about to prove it one more time!"

Epilogue

"This is Cassie Grant from Cassie's Night Calls making a daytime appearance here at WLVH Lovehandles, where love is more than just a song. We've used that slogan at Lovehandles since I started working here, and we proved it when Mary and Ethan married. And now we're proving it again.

"I'm here at our end of the summer 'Presque Isle Splash Bash' for a most unusual wedding of our very own. You might know the bride and groom as 'Punch and Judy in the morning,' but as soon as this ceremony is over, they'll be Peter and Judy O'Brien.

"I'll be with you all morning, here at the wedding, bringing you WLVH's second live ceremony. Speaking of weddings, they're starting the processional. Here come Judy's attendants out from one of the tents that line the beach. Ten pre-teens wearing their basketball uniforms. It might be unusual, but what did you expect of our Punch and Judy?

"And here comes the bride, wearing cut-off shorts and a WLVH t-shirt. Walking across the sand toward Erie's used-to-be most eligible bachelor. Sorry ladies, but Peter's dating days are over. Anyone here could tell you that this is a man who's only got eyes for one woman.

"Judy's reached Peter, and his band of college ushers—and let me tell you, these three are real cute, so you don't have to worry too much about Peter being off the market, there are some up and coming men around.

"I'm back a bit too far to hear their vows, but I can tell you that with the sun setting right behind them, this wedding along Lake Erie is one of the most romantic things I've ever seen. If you listen to my show, you'll know I'm a romantic through and through, and this takes the cake. Watching Peter and Judy find their own happily-ever-after.

"We've said WLVH Lovehandles is a place where love is more than just a song, and I think, with Peter and Judy's help, we've managed to prove it once again."